Float
Plan

Float

Plan

- - - - - - -

TRISH DOLLER

ST. MARTIN'S
GRIFFIN
NEW YORK

First published in the United States by St. Martin's Griffin,
an imprint of St. Martin's Publishing Group

FLOAT PLAN. Copyright © 2021 by Trish Doller. All rights reserved.
Printed in the United States of America. For information, address
St. Martin's Publishing Group, 120 Broadway, New York, NY 10271.

www.stmartins.com

Designed by Michelle McMillian

Library of Congress Cataloging-in-Publication Data

Names: Doller, Trish, author.
Title: Float plan / Trish Doller.
Description: First edition. | New York, NY : St. Martin's Griffin, 2021.
Identifiers: LCCN 2020042059 | ISBN 9781250767943 (trade paperback) |
    ISBN 9781250799760 (hardcover) | ISBN 9781250767950 (ebook)
Subjects: GSAFD: Love stories.
Classification: LCC PS3604.O4357 F58 2021 | DDC 813/.6—dc23
LC record available at https://lccn.loc.gov/2020042059

Our books may be purchased in bulk for promotional, educational, or business use.
Please contact your local bookseller or the Macmillan Corporate and
Premium Sales Department at 1-800-221-7945, extension 5442, or
by email at MacmillanSpecialMarkets@macmillan.com.

First Edition: 2021

10 9 8 7 6 5 4 3 2 1

In loving memory of Ms. Jean.
Miss you already.

Be advised, this novel contains discussions of self-harm and suicide.

The cure for anything is salt water—sweat, tears, or the sea.

—ISAK DINESEN

Float
Plan

Anna—

There's a kind of jacked-up happiness that comes when you know your life is almost over, when the decision to end it becomes solid. It might be adrenaline. It might be relief. And if I had always felt like this, I might have climbed mountains or raced marathons. Now it's just enough to see this through.

I should have left you alone that first night at the bar. If I had, you wouldn't be reading this letter at all. You'd be walking your dog or watching TV with your boyfriend. You didn't deserve to be dragged into my shit, and you definitely don't deserve the pain I'm about to cause. This is not your fault. For two years you have been my only reason for living. I wish I could give you forever.

You are strong and brave, and someday you'll be okay. You'll fall in love, and I hate him already for being a better man. Someday you will be happy again.

I love you, Anna. I'm sorry.
—Ben

ten months and six days (1)

I walk out of my life on Thanksgiving Day.

Last-minute shoppers are clearing shelves of stuffing mix and pumpkin pie filling as I heap my cart with everything I might need. (Dry beans. Canned vegetables. Rice.) I move through the grocery store like a prepper running late for doomsday. (Boxed milk. Limes. Spare flashlight.) I am quick so I won't lose my nerve. (Apples. Toilet paper. Red wine.) I try not to think beyond leaving. (Cabbage. Playing cards. Bottled water.) Or about what I might be leaving behind.

My mother calls as I'm wrangling the grocery bags into the back seat of my overstuffed Subaru. I haven't told her that I won't be there for Thanksgiving dinner, and she's not ready to hear that I'm skipping town. Not when I've barely left the house for the better part of a year. She'll have questions and I don't have answers, so I let the call go to voicemail.

When I reach the dock, the Alberg is right where it should

be, the shiny hull painted navy blue and the transom empty, still waiting for a name. For a moment I expect Ben's head to pop up from the companionway. I wait to see his little fuck-me grin, and to hear the excitement in his voice when he tells me today is the day. But the hatch is padlocked, and the deck is covered in bird shit—another part of my life I've let fall into neglect.

Ten months and six days ago, Ben swallowed a bottle of prescription Paxil and chased it with the cheap tequila that lived under the sink, and I don't know why. He was already gone when I came home from work and found him on the kitchen floor. In his suicide note, he told me I was his reason for living. Why was I not enough?

I breathe in deep, to the bottom of my lungs. Let it out slowly. Step onto the boat and unlock the hatch.

The air is stale and hot, smelling of wood wax, new canvas, and a hint of diesel. I haven't been aboard since before Ben died. Spiders have spun their homes in the corners of the cabin and a layer of dust has settled on every surface, but the changes leave me breathless. The interior brightwork is varnished and glossy. The ugly original brown-plaid cushion covers have been replaced with red canvas and Peruvian stripes. And a framed graphic hangs on the forward bulkhead that reads I & LOVE & YOU.

"Why do all this work for a trip you'll never take?" I say out loud, but it's another question without an answer. I wipe my eyes on the sleeve of my T-shirt. One of the things I've learned is that suicide doesn't break a person's heart just once.

It takes me the rest of the morning to clean the boat, unload the contents of my car, and stow everything away. Traces of Ben are everywhere: a saucepan at the bottom of the hanging locker, an expired six-pack of Heineken in the cockpit lazarette, a moldy orange life jacket stuffed in the refrigerator. I throw these things in the trash, but even with my spider plant hanging from an overhead handrail and my books lining the shelf, the boat belongs to Ben. He chose it. He did the renovations. He charted the course. He set the departure date. My presence feels like a layer as temporary as dust.

The last thing in my trunk is a shoebox filled with photos taken using Ben's old Polaroid, a dried hibiscus flower from our first date, a handful of dirty-sexy love letters, and a suicide note. I take out a single photo—Ben and me at the Hillsboro Inlet Lighthouse about a week before he died—and stash the box in the bottom drawer of the navigation station. I tape the photo to the wall in the V-berth, right above my pillow.

And it's time to go.

My only plan was to spend today in bed—my only plan since Ben's death—but I was startled out of sleep by an alarm. The notification on my phone said: TODAY IS THE DAY, ANNA! WE'RE GOING SAILING! Ben had programmed the event into my calendar almost three years ago—on the day he showed me his sailboat and asked me to sail the world with him—and I had forgotten. I cried until my eyelashes hurt, because there is no longer a *we* and I've forgotten how to be *me* without Ben. Then I got out of bed and started packing.

I've never been sailing without Ben. I don't always get the terminology correct—*it's a line, Anna, not a rope*—and I'll be lucky if I make it to the end of the river. But I am less afraid of what might become of me while sailing alone in the Caribbean than of what might become of me if I stay.

My boss calls as I'm untying the dock lines, no doubt wondering if I'm coming in, but I don't answer. He'll figure it out in a day or two.

I radio the drawbridge at Andrews Avenue for an opening, and slowly putter away from the dock, the engine chugging and choking after being silent for months. The current pulls me downriver as I guide the sailboat between the open bridge spans. Once I'm through, I'm passed by a large sportfishing boat. A guy wearing an aqua-colored fishing shirt waves to me from the back deck. He's no more than a couple of years older than I am, and good-looking in an outdoorsy, sun-bleached way. I wave back.

I motor past high-rise condos, sleek white mega-yachts, and a gridwork of canals lined with homes so large, my mother's house would barely fill the first floor. She's never been one to dream of mansions, but four people occupying a two-bedroom house is at least one too many. Mom says she loves having all her girls under one roof, but moving back home was not something I ever imagined. My life was supposed to be with Ben.

When I reach the drawbridge at Third Avenue, the tender tells me I'll have to wait because he just let a large sportfishing boat through. Ben always handled the boat when we had to wait, so I turn tight, timid circles—afraid of crashing into another waiting sailboat—until the cars stop and the bridge decks begin to lift.

At Port Everglades, cruise ships line the piers, their decks stacked like layers on a wedding cake. Cargo ships steam out through the cut into the Atlantic, destined for ports all over the world. The Alberg feels small and insignificant as I navigate between them, and I consider continuing safely south on the ICW instead of braving the open ocean. But the route in Ben's chart book would have me sail to Biscayne Bay before making the crossing to Bimini. So that is what I prepare to do.

I've tried to anticipate everything I might need at arm's length on the passage. I take quick stock as I slather on a fresh coat of sunscreen. Water. Snacks. Ben's raggedy straw cowboy hat that I clamp down on my head to shade my face. Cans of Coke. Hand-held VHF. Ditch bag in the closest cockpit locker, along with my life jacket and harness. Cell phone.

I'll be out of range soon, so I finally call my mother. "I wanted to let you know that I'm taking Ben's boat and going to sea for a while."

"Going to sea?" She snorts a little through her nose. "Anna, honey, what on earth are you talking about? It's Thanksgiving. The turkey is already in the oven."

"Today is the day that Ben and I were going to set out on our trip around the world," I explain. "I—I can't stay in Fort Lauderdale anymore. It hurts too much."

She's silent for such a long time that I think the call must have dropped.

"Mom?"

"This *ist* crazy, Anna. Crazy." My mom has lived in the United States longer than Rachel and I have been alive, but German words frequently slip into her speech, particularly when she's stressed. "You should not be going to sea in a boat you have no business trying to sail. You need to come home *und* get some help."

This isn't the first time we've had a conversation about me seeking professional help, but I don't need a therapist to tell me that I'm the only one who gets to decide how long my grief should last, that it's not my job to make other people less uncomfortable around me. I am *not* ready to get on with my life. I am *not* in the market for a new soul mate. And I'm *really* fucking tired of sharing a bedroom with my sister and a two-year-old.

"I'll check in when I get to the Bahamas." Behind me, a bright blue cargo freighter loaded high with shipping containers closes the distance between us. "I have to go, Mom, but I'm okay. Really. I'll call you from Bimini. *Ich liebe dich.*"

I slip the phone into the pocket of my shorts, feeling it vibrate with an incoming call as I hug the edge of the channel near the breakwater. Mom is probably calling back to talk some sense into me, and I suspect my phone will silently blow up until I lose the signal. But I can't worry about that when there's an enormous ship bearing down on me.

The freighter rumbles past, gulls wheeling and squabbling over the fish churned up in its wake. Sport fishers speed past. Other sailboats. The high-rise skyline of Fort Lauderdale recedes, and the sapphire Atlantic stretches off toward the horizon. The sea is languid, and the air is light.

It's a perfect day for running away from home.

Half a mile offshore, I turn the boat into the wind and put the engine in neutral. The mainsail raises easily enough, fluttering as it catches the breeze, but I'm not entirely sure the sail is all the way up the mast. Even after the jib is unfurled and the sails are trimmed, I don't know if I've done everything correctly. But the boat is moving in the proper direction. It's not on a collision course with any other vessel. Nothing is broken. I consider it a victory as I shut off the engine and settle back against a cushion for the six-hour sail to Miami.

These waters aren't completely unfamiliar. Ben and I once sailed to Miami and anchored for the night in the old marine stadium basin. Another time we spent the weekend at Biscayne National Park. Sailing to the Bahamas was going to be our first test to see if we could survive long-term living on a thirty-seven-foot boat. It seemed big until I went aboard the first time and saw that it was like a floating tiny house. Could Ben and I have managed living on top of each other? Would our relationship have lasted? The never-knowing is lodged in my heart like a stone, a constant dull ache that throbs during moments like these, when I wonder what our future might have been.

A bottlenose dolphin breaks the surface beside the boat, drawing me out of my head. I can't help but smile, remembering an argument we had about dolphins. Ben called them rapists and murderers. "Don't be fooled by their permanent smiles and happy chatter. They're assholes."

"Animals don't live by a moral code like humans," I countered. "So maybe you should be more outraged by actual rape than dolphins doing what dolphins do. Humans are the real assholes here."

He stared at me a long time, then flashed the grin that made my knees go wobbly. "God, Anna, how fucking lucky am I that you're mine?"

A second dolphin joins the first and they crisscross in front of the boat, playing chicken with the five-knot hull speed. They leap out of the water, showing off for each other, and it almost feels as though Ben sent them to me, which is ridiculous, but I watch them until they peel away, heading for wherever it is dolphins go.

"You were supposed to stay with me." My words float away on the breeze. "Why did you go somewhere I can't follow?"

Not sure if I'm talking to the dolphins or Ben. Either way, I get no response.

Sunset is fading into darkness when I motor the Alberg into a marina on the inside of Miami Beach. Ben circled No Name Harbor as our destination for the night, but I have never dropped anchor by myself, let alone in the dark. Instead I pinball the boat into a transient slip for the night, thankful there are no witnesses to my awful docking skills and badly tied knots.

Wearing one of Ben's old undershirts, I crawl into the V-berth and open the forward hatch. As I try to see the stars through the light pollution of Miami, I think about the last time Ben and I slept on the boat, one of the last times we made love. Sex is not what I miss most about him, but I do miss it. Before Ben, I had no idea that loneliness could ache in so many different places on a person's body.

Now I imagine him lying beside me. The warmth of his hands on my bare skin. The touch of his mouth against mine. Except the closer my imagination tries to draw him, the further away he feels.

aground (2)

The morning sun brushes across the back of my eyelids and I wake to the realization that I've overslept.

"Shit." I scramble out of the V-berth and hop across the cabin floor, pulling on a pair of cutoffs as I go. My plan was to leave Miami well before sunrise, so I'd reach Bimini while there was still daylight. "Shit. Shit. *Shit.*"

I quickly brush my teeth and braid my hair, then walk to the marina office, where I pay an ungodly sum for what might have been my last good night of sleep. Feeling the pinch of being behind schedule, I hurry back to the boat, cast off the lines, and narrowly miss crashing into a seventy-foot cruiser on my way out of the dock.

"You're lucky you didn't hit my boat," a man says from the back deck. His eyes are hidden behind sunglasses, but his mouth is bracketed by disapproval.

"Trust me," I say, my face burning with embarrassment. "I'm aware."

I motor down Government Cut, past the cruise ships and ferries and out into the ocean, where I raise the sails and aim the boat toward the compass heading marked on Ben's chart.

Had I undertaken this trip aboard a powerboat, I would already be in Bimini. I'd be lying on the beach, browsing the local shops, or sipping a fruity cocktail in a waterfront bar. I would have plowed right across the Gulf Stream and arrived a couple of hours later. But sailing to Bimini is an all-day endeavor.

Ben and I used to take turns driving the boat, but without him, I don't feel comfortable walking away. I can't go down into the cabin for some respite from the sun or to use the toilet. I can't read a book. And the passage between Florida and the Bahamas is a busy shipping lane of tankers and container ships heading north to ports in the United States and Europe, and south toward the Panama Canal.

The wind is too light. The Alberg is only making about four knots. I struggle to stay alert as the sun moves across the sky. I jerk awake to find myself veering off course, the sails backwinded and flapping. Desperate, I pour water down the front of my tank top, but it's not cold enough to shock my skin. I drink a lukewarm Coke, hoping for a caffeine jolt. Cue up a playlist of the most screaming punk rock I can find and sing at the top of my lungs. Anything to stay awake when my overheated system wants to stall out.

The next time I wake, it's to the splash of a container ship passing within a dozen yards of the boat, its hull rising like a huge steel wall. So close that I can see a deckhand watching me from the stern. The Alberg pitches lightly on the wake. If the captain saw me, I don't know. If he sounded the horn, I didn't hear it. My heart slams against my chest and my entire body is shaking as I put the sailboat back on its proper course.

You should not be going to sea in a boat you have no business trying to sail.

Fear and shame bubble up inside me as my mother's words echo in my head. I could have been killed, crashed into by a cargo ship bound for Cartagena. If I can't manage fifty miles to Bimini, how will I ever make the long passage from the Turks and Caicos to Puerto Rico? Mom is right. I should go home.

And do what, exactly?

I walked out on my job. And the apartment where I lived with Ben now belongs to a couple of snowbirds from New Jersey. Even the vastness of the blue sea surrounding me feels less empty than the prospect of a life without him.

* * *

The night we met, he was sitting at the end of the bar, a nautical chart book spread out in front of him and a bottle of Red Stripe beside his sun-stained arm. I didn't know yet that it was a chart book. I only knew that it was not normal for someone to set up shop in a pirate-themed restaurant where the waitresses were dressed like tavern wenches.

Carla, my best friend, was slicing limes as I came on shift. The daytime staff was supposed to leave the bar fully stocked for the night crew—a favor we returned at closing—but she always left the garnish prep until the last minute.

"What's with the architect?" I picked up a paring knife and began cutting a lemon into wedges, even though it was her job.

Usually I worked the floor with the other waitresses, but I'd been covering for Denise, who was out on maternity leave.

"It's a map," Carla said. "He's sailing around the world or something. I don't know. He's cute, but I stopped listening. He'd be perfect for you, though."

"What? Why?"

She shoulder-bumped me. "Because you, Anna Beck, are in desperate need of a little seaman in your life."

"Oh my God." I cracked up laughing and glanced over to make sure he hadn't heard. His focus was on the chart book as though nothing else in the room existed. "You are the worst."

Carla leaned over and kissed my cheek. "But you love me, right?"

"I'd love you more if you stayed to do the oranges."

"I have a date and I smell like a beer tap exploded in my face . . . because a beer tap exploded in my face," she said, stuffing the lime wedges into the garnish caddy. "So I'm going to have to take my chances with your love."

"Should I wait up?" I shared an apartment with Carla and two other waitresses from the restaurant. Like flight attendant crash pads, the apartment mostly served as a place to sleep and I don't think all four of us were ever there at the same time.

"I wouldn't," she said with a grin.

"Don't forget to use a condom!" I called after her, but Carla was impossible to embarrass. She blew me a kiss as she left, calling back, "I plan on using several!"

Lemon wedges complete, I dried my hands and worked my way down the bar, checking on customers. Introducing myself. Pouring fresh beers. Finally I reached map guy. "Ready for another drink?"

"I'm good, thanks," he said, his concentration fixed on the chart book in front of him. But he glanced up, and our eyes met. His were dark brown and soft, like you could tumble into them and land safely. "Oh, uh, yeah. I guess I'm having another Red Stripe."

"Okay, then."

"Please," he added as I turned toward the cooler, and that one polite word did me in. It sounds ridiculous, improbable, and so patently absurd that I could fall in love with someone at first sight. But when I returned to him with a fresh bottle of beer, he gave me my very first Ben Braithwaite fuck-me grin—completely oblivious to its knee-weakening effect—and I knew right then he was going to be part of my world.

"I'm Anna, by the way."

"Ben." He reached across the bar to shake my hand. Carla was not wrong. He was cute in a boyish surfer-dude way. Definitely my type. His caramel-colored hair hung almost to his shoulders and looked so soft that I wanted to run my fingers through it.

Instead I gestured at the chart, which had a pencil line running from Florida to one of the islands in the Bahamas. "What-cha working on there, Ben?"

"I just bought an old boat, an Alberg," he said, and his face lit up like a kid on Christmas morning. "It needs a bunch of work, but my plan is to fix it up and sail around the— Um, someone down the bar is trying to get your attention."

"Oops. I work here, don't I? Hold that thought. I'll be back."

He smiled, but those dark eyes were serious. "I'm not going anywhere."

That was the thing about Ben. He had no guile, no game. He

was always earnest and sweet, and from the very beginning he offered me his whole heart.

* * *

The sky is dark when I reach Bimini, the pink-and-gold sunset long gone below the horizon. I hate sailing into an unfamiliar harbor in the dark, but I have no one to blame but myself. Nosing the boat to the wind, I roll up the jib and lower the mainsail. After thirteen hours at sea, my body is sore. My face feels as if it's been stretched, burned by both sun and wind. And after taking down my shorts twice in the middle of the ocean to pee into the scupper drain, I'm ready for a hot shower.

Using Ben's spotlight, I scan the water for navigational markers as I approach the channel that cuts between North and South Bimini. It's hard to see anything in the dark and there is very little ambient light coming off the islands. The Alberg stutters when the keel drags along the bottom and my heart stutters along with it.

"No!" I throw the tiller over, trying to steer in the direction of what I hope is the middle of the channel, but the boat comes to a complete stop. "I am not running aground right now!"

I shift the engine into reverse, hoping to back myself out of this mess, but nothing happens. The sound that escapes me is a cross between hysterical laughter and sobbing. I am so close to land that I could jump out of the boat and wade ashore.

"Fuck."

I burrow around the lazarette for my phone to look up the tide table, but there's no signal. Likely for the best—I don't want to know how many texts and calls I've missed. I drop the useless phone back into the locker and pray the tide is incoming. Otherwise, this will be a long, long night.

Since the boat isn't going anywhere for a while, I climb down into the galley and make a turkey sandwich—the closest I'm going to get to Thanksgiving dinner. My mom is probably hurt that I won't be there, and I think again about giving up this impulsive plan. Once I come unstuck, I could return to Florida. Beg for my job back. Live on the boat. Fake it till I make it. That would be fine, wouldn't it? Except Ben wasn't content with fine; he wanted extraordinary. Shouldn't I want the same?

If he were here, he would laugh at my embarrassment over running aground and say, "If no one saw you do it, did it really happen?" He'd hang a solar lamp from the boom, crack open a cold beer, and cue up a playlist of his favorite sailing music. He'd turn the moment into a party. When I finish eating my sandwich, I do all of those things, performing them like a summoning ritual that might bring him back.

They never do.

Without Ben, it's too much. I switch off the music after a handful of songs and listen to the quiet, rhythmic *shh-shh-shh* of waves lapping against the shore. Except thinking about him makes me restless. I stand up and move from one side of the cockpit to the other, rocking the boat, hoping the seafloor will loosen its grip. I feel ridiculous, but suddenly the boat shifts. It begins to drift, pushed forward on the current. I quickly start the engine and steer back into the deeper part of the channel, where I stay until I reach the anchorage.

There aren't many boats as I stand on the bow to throw the anchor into the water, a relief because I don't know how much line to let out, and even when it feels secure, I don't have the expertise to tell when the anchor is holding fast. I turn on the anchor light at the top of the mast and hoist the yellow quarantine flag so customs officials will know I haven't cleared into the Bahamas yet.

The last thing I do as I crawl into the V-berth—still wearing my clothes—is say a prayer to God, Ben, and the universe that the anchor won't drag in the night, that when I wake tomorrow morning, the boat won't be smashed against the shore.

drunken kaleidoscope (3)

The sky is a faded blue when I wake, one that could mean dawn or dusk. The travel clock on the shelf beside my head reads 6:09. No help at all. It seems impossible that I could have slept all night and through most of another day, but when I climb out into the cockpit, the leading edge of the sun has met the horizon. The sunset sky is slashed with red and purple, like the work of a painter with an angry brush. Except, the saying goes "red sky at night, sailor's delight," so this is promising. Tomorrow should be a good weather day.

The boat did not drift while I slept. It didn't swing in the current and hit any other boats, either. A minor miracle. I walk up to the bow to double-check last night's half-assed handiwork. Whenever we anchored somewhere together, Ben would wake every couple of hours to make sure the anchor was holding. Too much swing and he'd bolt out of bed, sure we were drifting. My relief leaches out of me, replaced by guilt. I should have been paying attention. Ben would have.

But the anchor is doing its thing, and I feel more rested than I have in months.

And hungry.

Rowing the dinghy to shore for dinner on a tropical island sounds appealing. Reggae music from one of the waterfront bars floats across the water, but I've missed office hours for customs. Maybe no one would notice, but I'm not prepared to break any laws that might come with a hefty fine. Instead I pour a glass of red wine and make no-meat spaghetti that I eat straight from the pan.

Tomorrow I'll go to the customs and immigration office, and I'll find a way to call my mom. She's probably going out of her mind with worry, but my cell phone still has no signal and there's no free Wi-Fi floating on the breeze with Bob Marley.

Tomorrow I'll decide what I'm going to do about the day after tomorrow. Crossing from Miami was the easiest part and I fucked it up. Do I gamble that my accidental good fortune will hold through an entire archipelago?

Tonight I wash the dishes and lie on the foredeck, looking up at the night sky and remembering the time Ben and I did this together. He pointed at a constellation. I don't remember which one, only that we were anchored in a mangrove-filled bay in Key Largo where the sky was so exploded with stars, it felt like the whole universe was at our fingertips.

"There," he said. "That little star at the bottom. That one is yours, Anna. Forever and always."

I didn't remind him that sometimes the light we see is left over from dead stars. It couldn't be mine if it was already gone.

Had I paid better attention to where he was pointing, I might be able to find that star tonight. But it doesn't matter. I already know how it feels to try holding on to the light of a dead star.

* * *

My second morning in Bimini dawns so bright, I have no idea how I could have slept through yesterday, but today I'm wide-awake. I inflate the dinghy and row to the marina, where there is a customs office. I bring along my passport, boat registration, customs paperwork, and cash for the cruising fee. Ben and I read horror stories about officials in the Caribbean expecting bribes or adding on "taxes" because no one has the authority to stop them, but the Bahamian officers are all business as they stamp my passport and accept my cash.

Officially cleared, I go back to the boat, where I take a fast shower. After I'm dried and dressed, my hair braided, I lock up the cabin and go ashore.

The island's main road is lined with sherbet-hued shops, bars, restaurants, and homes, and there are more cars than I expected for an island that's only seven miles long and several hundred feet wide. Bimini reminds me of a favorite toy, shabby and worn, but well loved. I step into a tiny blue grocery store, where I buy a SIM card so my phone will work in the Bahamas. My first call is home.

"Oh, thank God." Relief floods my mother's voice, but I hear Rachel muttering in the background. Sometimes it's like having two mothers, like I'm five instead of twenty-five. "I called the coast guard to report you missing, but they said there was nothing they could do if you'd left the country."

"I'm sorry I didn't call sooner," I say. "I arrived really late the night before last and slept about fifteen hours straight. I only just came ashore and got my cell phone sorted out."

"I don't understand this, Anna. What you are doing is foolish."

I didn't call to fight with her, but my defenses go up. "You're the one who keeps telling me it's time to move on."

"But that is not what's happening," my mother says. "You are sailing Ben's boat, living his dreams. You are not putting him in the past; you're wallowing in his memory."

"Maybe I need to wallow."

"Anna, it's been almost a year."

"I wasn't aware there was an expiration date for grief."

"That's not what I mean. You should talk to a therapist." She sniffles and I realize she is crying, and I feel even worse. "I've never had to worry about you, and now that's all I ever do."

"I'm sorry."

"I don't want you to be sorry, *Liebchen;* I want you to be happy. Ben would want you to be happy."

One of the worst things about life after Ben is how everyone seems to be able to predict what he would want. *He'd want you to start dating. He'd want you to be happy.*

"Yeah, well," I say, "his death pretty much sealed the deal on the exact opposite."

"Please come home."

"I can't."

Mom breaks down in tears and I hear Rachel huff as she takes the phone. I steel myself for the oncoming storm. "Anna, you need to knock this shit off. Think about someone other than yourself for a change."

As kids, Rachel and I were close. Barely two years apart, we played together, went to school together. Until he left, Dad called us his two little peas in a pod. But after Rachel had Maisie, something changed. Sometimes I get a jealous vibe, but I don't understand why. Rachel has a job she loves and a beautiful child. I have a gaping hole where my life used to be.

"Tell Mom I'll call her in a few days." I disconnect and silence my phone.

The crossing from Florida was definitely not an unequivocal success—not when I overslept, nearly got smeared by a cargo ship, and ran aground only a few yards from my destination—but maybe I've gotten all the foolishness out of the way. Maybe I can handle island hopping through the rest of the Bahamas and the Caribbean.

Except the passage from the Turks and Caicos to Puerto Rico is about four hundred miles of open seas, battered by trade winds. There is no shortcut. And there is absolutely no way I can do it alone. I need to find someone to help me.

At the marina there is a bulletin board pinned with business cards for diving charters and rain-faded flyers for fishing tournaments. I leave a note that says:

WANTED: EXPERIENCED CREW TO ASSIST
ON PASSAGE FROM TURKS AND CAICOS
TO PUERTO RICO. SALARY NEGOTIABLE,
MEALS INCLUDED. TEXT 555-625-6470
FOR MORE INFORMATION.

Jangling with nervous energy, I leave the resort complex, heading south. The island is fully awake and busy with tourists buzzing around on golf carts and locals calling out greetings to one another as they walk down the main road. I turn onto a shorter street that cuts across the narrow island and end up at a cluster of tiny beachfront restaurants. A group of young men are hanging out around the doorway to one of the shops, talking loudly, drinking beer, and listening to the dance music that spills from speakers mounted on stands along the side of the building. Beyond the restaurants is the beach, where people have spread out their blankets. A dog rolls in the sand and children play in an ocean that's so vivid—seafoam green and turquoise and cobalt—it hardly seems real.

I step inside a restaurant called CJ's, where I order an egg sandwich for lunch and grab a beer from the cooler.

"You can wait out back," the woman behind the counter tells me. "We'll call you when your food is ready."

Behind the building is a wooden deck with picnic tables overlooking the beach. A couple of guys are drinking Heinekens and talking, but their accents are moving too fast for me to understand what they're saying. I snap a picture of the beach with my phone, then sit on a bench beneath a shady pine to wait for my lunch. *Content* isn't exactly the word I'd use for how I feel, but Bimini makes me feel a little bit lighter, a little bit hopeful. Right now an egg sandwich and a beer are all I need.

* * *

After lunch I buy a second beer and step down from the deck onto the sand. All around me, people are together. Families. Couples. Groups of college students who probably came over on the fast ferry. I wade out into the water and pretend it's totally fine that I'm alone on a tropical island in the middle of a sparkling ocean.

As waves wash against my shins, a brown-skinned boy no older than eight or nine, wearing dripping brown cutoffs that hang around his narrow hips, approaches me with a fistful of plastic dive sticks. "Will you throw these for us?"

Behind him, other kids watch me with expectant faces. One little girl in a bright pink bathing suit hops on one foot, trying to keep her balance on the shifting sand. Another boy bobs his head, as if willing me to say yes.

"Sure." I take the sticks, step a little deeper into the water, and fling them as hard as I can. The whole pack of children shriek and race into the water. They dive under, their feet churning the surface. One boy comes up with two. A girl with one. The first boy has the remaining three, held high above his head like a trophy. It reminds me of when my sister and I would dive for pennies at the bottom of motel pools when we went on vacation. The winner was the one who collected the most and Rachel almost always won.

"Again, please?" the boy asks.

"Ellis!" a woman calls from a nearby blanket. "Don't be bothering the lady. She doesn't need to entertain you."

"I don't mind," I say, accepting the sticks from Ellis. I throw them again, and while the kids are thrashing around in the surf, I head back up to CJ's for another beer.

At the order counter there are three white men dressed in pastel fishing shirts, swim trunks, and visors. The light-blue-shirted one sees me take a beer from the cooler. Of the three, he is closest to my age. He flashes a wide grin and says, "Let me get that for you."

And suddenly I'm incredibly angry at Ben. I know he tried to manage his depression. When we met, he'd been struggling most of his life to find a mix of medications that worked. But if he was suicidal, why didn't he get help? Why didn't he tell me? This was supposed to be us, together, not me on my own.

Fuck you, Ben Braithwaite.

I haven't picked up a guy in a long time, but it's ridiculously easy. All I have to do is hand him the bottle of beer, smile, and say, "Thank you so much. I'm Anna."

"Nice to meet you, Anna. I'm Chris." His nose is peeling, freckled, and really fucking adorable. In fact, he's covered in pale brown freckles. "This is Doug." He gestures toward the guy in the pink shirt. Oldest. Mid-to-late thirties. Wedding band. "And Mike." Yellow shirt. Thinning hair. Hot in a generic dumb guy sort of way.

ChrisDougMike. They're pretty interchangeable, like most of the guys who used to come into the pirate bar. But I like the soft, knee-wobbling way Chris says my name. And there's a freckle on the bottom edge of his lower lip that dangles like tempting fruit. Also, I'm a little tipsy. He sees me staring at his mouth and gives me a cocky grin.

"So, what brings you to Bimini?" he asks as we move to a picnic table on the deck. He sits beside me.

"Sailboat."

He laughs. "Just you?"

I nod. "Yep. I left Fort Lauderdale on Thursday."

"Wait." His blue eyes narrow as he studies me. "Were you on a blue boat on the river?"

"Yep."

"I knew I'd seen that blond hair before." He runs his fingers down the length of one of my braids and gives the end a gentle tug. The gesture is prematurely intimate, but we're already on a collision course. "I waved when we passed you."

"Oh, right," I say, smiling. "You were the reason I had to wait ten minutes at the Third Avenue Bridge so they could let some traffic pass."

"Sorry." His twisty little smirk says he's not sorry at all. "I hope it doesn't change your opinion of me."

"What do you think my opinion is?"

"Well." He takes a long pull from his bottle and I watch his Adam's apple move as he swallows. "You were interested enough to let me buy you a beer. You've already contemplated kissing me." My face gets warm and the smirk reappears. "You think I have potential, so I don't want to mess up my chances."

"At what?"

"Whatever you'll let me get away with."

The afternoon slips away as we take turns buying rounds of beer. ChrisDougMike are all Canadians who have jobs in sales— car dealership, liquor distributor, insurance company—and came to Bimini to catch wahoo. They talk about rods and reels, retelling fishing stories I won't remember tomorrow, and Chris inches closer and closer. I stop caring about talking when our bare knees make contact beneath the table. Our elbows touch. Arms. Shoulders. As if we're melting into each other.

At some point, Doug and Mike go down to the beach, leaving

us alone. Chris leans over, his lips grazing my neck, my ear, setting off a shower of sparks under my skin.

"You want to get out of here?" he whispers. "I have a room."

For the first time since he died, I don't think about what Ben would want. He's not the little voice inside my head urging me to go, go, go. And he's definitely not in the warm ache between my thighs. Chris's callused palm slides under the hem of my sundress, stroking the inside of my knee.

"Anna." A gentle squeeze.

"Yes. Let's go."

The walk from the beach to the resort is a drunken kaleidoscope, scattered bits of need and tumbling shards of shame. My back pressed against the wall of an out-of-business clothing shop with Chris's mouth on my neck and his fingers inside my bikini bottom, making me gasp. Running. Losing a flip-flop. Tumbling backward onto his bed. The feel of his mouth, his tongue, on all the places that haven't been touched in months by anyone but me. Hot, sticky, mindless want.

My legs are still trembling when Chris gets out of bed, naked, to get a condom from his carry-on. His phone vibrates on the bedside table as he tears open the foil packet. The screen is alive with a photo of him kissing a pretty blonde dressed in a wedding gown. Shit.

"Anna, wait."

My name no longer sounds beautiful and, God, I am so gullible. Ben never lied to me or played games. So it never occurred to me that Chris might be married, or that it was even a question I needed to ask. If I had, would he have told me the truth?

I snatch my dress off the hotel room floor and yank it over

my head while Chris stands in the bathroom doorway, looking from me to his ringing phone and back, as if he still has a choice. As if there is anything he could say that would convince me to stay. My bikini is lost in the bedding, so I leave it behind with my one remaining flip-flop and an enormous piece of my dignity.

I glance back at Chris as I step through the doorway. "Go fuck yourself."

I stumble through the resort grounds to the end of the dock where my dinghy is tied. I climb down a ladder to the little boat, where I sit for . . . I have no idea how long, listening miserably to the happy sounds of an island not ready to sleep. I ran away from Fort Lauderdale because I wasn't ready to move on, yet threw myself at the first man who asked. I feel dirty. Unfaithful.

I'm so, so sorry, Ben. Please forgive me.

I want to row out to the boat, pull up the anchor, and sail away from this place, but I'm not sober enough for any of that. And Bimini isn't really the problem. Instead I curl up on the floor of the dinghy and cry.

question mark (4)

I wake in the V-berth of the Alberg as if last night was nothing more than a bad dream, except there's a spike of pain splitting my skull and I have no recollection of how I ended up in my own bed. Shifting the comforter aside, I discover I'm wearing yesterday's sundress. The soles of my feet are filthy, my mouth tastes like I might have vomited, and my bikini is completely gone. I can remember my walk of shame and crying in the dinghy, but beyond that, the night ends in a question mark.

I'm relishing the small relief of being safe when I hear the cabin floor creak and catch a whiff of . . . coffee? I roll over to see a dark-haired man leaning against the galley sink, drinking from Ben's favorite Captain America mug. Part of me wants to leap from my bed and snatch it away because that mug belongs to *Ben*, but the bigger, more rational part of me is trying to figure out why there is a stranger on the boat. He's not riffling through cabinets like a thief searching for valuables. He looks relaxed, comfortable, as though he was invited. Did I invite him?

The scene jumps to the next level of unexpected when I notice that the lower half of his right leg—from his knee down into his black Adidas sneaker—is bionic and complicated-looking. Not flesh and bone.

I have no idea what's happening.

"Um . . . hello?"

He turns in my direction and, under any other circumstances, waking up to this man's face would probably be a religious experience. He looks like he should be playing guitar and singing in pubs, with dark just-fucked hair and a scruffy jawline. "Oh good," he says. "You're awake."

"Who are you?"

"You don't remember?" He touches his hand to his heart, covering up the crackled gold letters that spell CIARRAÍ across the chest of his faded green T-shirt. He's older than I am by a handful of years, but his grin is pure ten-year-old boy with a frog behind his back. And his accent sounds Irish. "Now you've gone and shattered my heart."

I sit up and swing my legs over the edge of my bed. After my narrow miss with a married man, there's no way I would've had sex with a different stranger. I think. "Did we . . . ?"

"Christ, no." He pours a second mug of coffee. Mine, with flowers and the pink A for Anna. "You were drunker than a monkey, but I did appreciate the offer."

"Oh my God."

"I'm joking." He closes the space between us and offers me the mug. Accepting a drink—even a caffeinated one—from a strange man is not a mistake I should make twice, but the coffee smells good, and I desperately need it. I take it.

"The long and short of it is this—I found you passed out in your dinghy and it wouldn't have been right to leave you there with your bare arse for God and all of Bimini to see." His accent grows more pronounced as he picks up speed. "So, I rowed you out here to your boat and helped you to bed, then realized I was stranded unless I took your dinghy, in which case you'd be stranded. I slept on deck. I hope you don't mind that I borrowed a sleeping bag."

As if everything about last night wasn't already deeply embarrassing, this man has seen my ass. He also saved me from . . . well, who knows what could have happened while I was unconscious and half-naked. Someone else, someone less honorable, could have found me first. He rescued me from that possibility—and my own stupidity.

"Wow, um—thank you for being so kind."

He rubs a hand over his messy hair and glances down at the floor before looking at me. "Well, I didn't want to see you come to any harm, is all."

"And it's not that I'm not completely grateful, because I am, but . . . who are you?"

"Oh, right. Keane Sullivan."

"Anna." I opt not to overshare on the personal details. Lord knows what I might have said last night when I was drunk. "How did you guess which boat was mine?"

"There was only one without a dinghy," Keane says with a one-shouldered shrug. "The odds seemed favorable."

"Well, thank you. For everything." I take a sip of coffee and steal a quick glance at my phone to see if anyone responded to my job offer while I was off making bad choices. There's a notification, and a string of digits that don't look anything like a telephone number. The text says: I am a professional sailor and delivery captain currently in Bimini. If you haven't already filled the position, I'm interested.

"Excuse me one second," I say, typing a quick response.

I haven't filled the position.

"Are you hungry?" Keane asks, digging into his back pocket. He pulls out his phone and looks at the screen. "My apologies. I've got to check this." He quickly taps out a message as he talks. "Whenever I'm hungover, fried eggs and buttered toast usually set me to rights."

The thought of food makes my stomach queasy, and this man has done more for me than anyone should have had to do. "I don't know if—" My phone chimes with a new text.

Meet me at the Big Game restaurant in an hour? I'll be wearing a green shirt. I'm Keane, by the way.

My shoulders shake with suppressed laughter as I respond.

You'll probably recognize me by my ass.

Keane looks down at his phone, and up at me, laughter escaping him in a great gust. We laugh until I have tears in my eyes and my sides ache. I haven't laughed this much since before Ben died. The sound withers in my throat because . . . shit . . . I'm not ready for this. I didn't think about having to share the boat with someone, even for a few days. Keane is taller and broader, and his presence takes up so much space. My second thoughts have second thoughts.

Keane notices. "Doing okay there, Anna?"

"I, um—"

He hands me a worn, folded piece of paper, his résumé, a two-page list of boats he's crewed aboard and yacht deliveries he's done. Ben bought a boat before he knew how to sail it, but Keane . . . he's sailed all over the world, even raced across the wild Southern Ocean.

"Listen, if it's the leg, I assure you I'm more capable with one than most people are with two," he says without a hint of swagger. "I can get you to Puerto Rico."

"It's not the leg. Truly," I say, as I hand back his résumé. There's a just-rightness about Keane Sullivan that is comforting. He feels like someone I can trust. "I mean, what you did for me last night proves you're the perfect person for the job, but I didn't think this through. Since leaving Florida, I've made a series of bad decisions and I need to consider whether continuing this trip would be one more."

He nods as he folds the list back up and shoves it into his pocket. "I understand. If you change your mind, you have my number."

"Thanks again," I say.

"Think nothing of it, Anna," Keane says. "Would you mind giving me a lift back to the dock?"

Carla once told me that the best way to make a decision is to flip a coin. She said that when the coin is in the air, you'll usually figure out what you truly want. There's no spinning coin here, but as Keane turns to climb the companionway ladder, I realize that if I let him leave, I will not find anyone better. And I don't really want to go home.

"I've changed my mind about those eggs."

* * *

Keane plows into his breakfast as though he's being clocked for speed. His cheek is stuffed with food as he tells me how he left home in County Kerry, Ireland, when he was only seventeen.

"My older brothers were footballers and hurlers, but I was drawn to the sea and loved mucking around in boats," he says, smearing red currant jelly on his toast. "As soon as I was able to swim, my mom signed me up for sailing lessons at our town club and that's all I've ever done."

"So, you just . . . sail?"

"Essentially. I began as crew on local boats for fun, then team raced for the College of Charleston in South Carolina and worked my way onto yachts that were seriously campaigning," he says. "Built something of a reputation as a world-class bowman and became a hired gun for anyone who wanted to win races."

"Oh, um—we should probably talk about pay."

"That was not meant to be a segue," Keane says, gesturing at me with his fork before stabbing a piece of egg. "But listen . . . I need to get to Puerto Rico, so if you're willing to give me a lift, I'll do the job for free."

"Are you sure?"

He nods. "Absolutely. To be honest, I'm eager to have a sail on this gorgeous boat. How did you come by it?"

"My boyfriend found it in a boatyard in Fort Lauderdale."

"The one in the photo?" Keane gestures toward the V-berth.

"Yes."

"Why is he not making this trip with you, if you don't mind my asking?"

I'm afraid to answer his question because I don't want to see Keane change into someone who treats me as though I'm made of glass. Despite my bad judgment last night, he has treated me like an unbroken person. But I need to be honest so that if I come unglued, he'll know why.

"He's, um—Ten months ago he died by suicide."

He looks up, hazel eyes wide. "Jesus, that fucking sucks."

A laugh escapes me, and I flatten my hand over my mouth, horrified at myself. There's nothing funny about Ben's death, but Keane's reaction catches me off guard. Tears sting my eyes and the world gets blurry.

"When I lost my leg," he says, "people kept apologizing. I know they were genuinely sorry that I'd experienced such a terrible trauma, but I got so bloody tired of hearing it. Just once I hoped someone would say, 'Jesus, that fucking sucks.'"

"It really does suck." I scrub my eyes with the heels of my hands. This time I laugh because I'm embarrassed that he's managed to see me only at my worst. "Thank you."

"You're welcome." There's a light of understanding in his eyes, and for the first time in months, I don't feel like a moldy unidentifiable lump in the back of someone's refrigerator. I feel seen.

"When were you thinking of leaving Bimini?" Keane asks.

"As soon as possible."

*　*　*

Taking a shower makes me feel human again, and while Keane takes the dinghy to get his things from the yacht he delivered yesterday from Key West, I catch up on the phone messages I've been ignoring.

My mom's voicemails are alternately angry and weepy, demanding that I call her back, then begging me to come home. Listening makes me heartsore. Her life hasn't been easy. Dad dragged her to the States as a military bride and then walked out when my sister and I were kids. I've tried so hard to not give her reason to worry, but I don't possess her German stoicism. I can't pretend my grief doesn't exist.

There's a missed call from my boss, informing me I've officially been fired. And a second call to remind me that if I don't return my uniforms, I'll be charged for them.

Finally, there's a voicemail from Ben's mother. She barely spoke to me when her son was alive, and after his death, she gave me one week's notice to move out of his apartment. Swept me away like trash. She's left several voicemails in the past few weeks, but I've deleted them all, just like I delete this one.

Instead of calling my mom, I send her an email, explaining that I've hired a reputable guide to travel with me to Puerto Rico. *Try not to worry too much*, I write. *I'll call when I get to San Juan. Ich liebe dich.*

The dishes are washed and stowed, and my bed is made, when I hear my name. I climb out of the cabin as Keane maneuvers the dinghy alongside the sailboat. With one hand he passes up an enormous yellow duffel bag that's so heavy, I stagger backward.

"Jesus," I say. "Is this thing filled with rocks?"

He laughs. "No, just all my worldly possessions."

"Really?"

"Aye." He hands me the oars, and climbs onto the boat, hauling the dinghy up behind him. I've seen people with prosthetic legs who need canes or crutches, but Keane moves with the fluid grace of someone who knows his way around boats—prosthesis or otherwise. "And lately I've been thinking it's time to downsize."

As I pull the plug to deflate the dinghy, I don't tell him my entire wardrobe is crammed into this boat, including a pair of strappy sandals in the hanging locker and a bronze sequined skirt folded into a drawer. He doesn't need to know that I'm a messed-up girl flying by the seat of her pants. He'll find out soon enough.

so fucking unfair (5)

Sailing with someone to spell you when you're tired or need to pee is a vastly different experience from sailing alone. Keane and I create a four-hour watch rotation, giving each of us time to eat or nap or read a book. On his first watch, Keane sends a fishing line out from the stern, trolling for whatever might take a bite. Bimini is fading into the horizon.

I am down in the cabin, trying to decide what to make for dinner, when the line starts whizzing off the reel and Keane's fishing rod bends in an arc.

"Anna," he calls. "A little help, please?"

I take over the tiller while he picks up the pole to do battle with the fish on the other end of the line.

"Could be a barracuda or perhaps a small shark." His biceps strain as he cranks on the reel, pulling the fish closer and closer. When it reaches the boat, the fish is a silver blur beneath the surface, thrashing wildly, fighting its fate. As Keane lands it on the cockpit floor, it writhes and flops, gills gaping in the air.

"What is it?" I ask.

"Mackerel." He reaches for the winch handle and I wince as he gives the fish a sharp smack on the head to kill it. Keane trades the handle for a fillet knife and slices the mackerel from top to tail. Inside, the heart is still pulsing, unaware that the fish is dead. "Want a bite?"

"What? Now?"

"Sashimi doesn't get any fresher," he says, offering me a ragged sliver of raw fish.

The flesh is warm and minerally on my tongue, nothing like the cool, tidy rolls at my favorite sushi bar. Here we have no little bowls of soy sauce or decorative mounds of wasabi, just a cockpit that looks like a crime scene. I eat a second piece, and a third, feeling slightly *Lord of the Flies*. "I thought this was going to be terrible, but—"

"Incredible, right?" Keane says, separating the meat from the skin. He tosses the offal overboard. "I'll portion a bit out for dinner and put the rest in your freezer for another day."

He gathers up the remaining fish and carries it down to the galley, while I use my dishwashing bucket to rinse down the cockpit. When he comes back to resume his watch, I stay on deck.

"Where in Ireland are you from?"

"You probably haven't heard of it, but a small town on the southwest coast called Tralee," Keane says. "The closest town people know is Killarney."

"I haven't heard of Killarney, either, so . . ."

He laughs. "You're from Florida?"

"Born and raised in Fort Lauderdale."

"What do you do there?"

"Are you familiar with Hooters?"

Keane glances at me, but his eyes are shaded behind aviator-style sunglasses, so I have no idea what he might be thinking. "As a concept, yes, but I've never been."

"The place I worked was like Hooters, but with a pirate theme," I explain. "The waitresses dressed like sexy pirates and the bartenders wore black tank tops with the word *wench* across the back."

"Did you enjoy it?"

"When you work in a restaurant like that, people tend to think you're either flaunting it and you think too highly of yourself, or you're degrading yourself and you have low self-esteem," I say, thinking of the little side comments Ben's mother used to make. "There's very little accounting for how most of the women are simply trying to pay bills or support their families in a patriarchal system that doesn't seem to be going away anytime soon. I'm not thrilled with being objectified, but I've made a lot of money letting it happen, so my feelings are complicated."

"Mine too. I'm not certain I'd feel entirely comfortable eating in a place where it feels like the staff is part of the menu, but sexy pirates?" Keane grins. "I wouldn't hate it either."

"That's fair." I stand and head toward the companionway. "I'm grabbing a Coke. Would you like one?"

"I would, thanks . . . wench."

I give him the finger and his laughter follows me down into the cabin. I open the refrigerator hatch, my eye catching on the bulkhead wall. I & LOVE & YOU. Sadness tumbles me like a wave, and I climb into the V-berth to look at Ben's photo.

The morning we snapped that Polaroid, he woke me when it was still dark, whispering, "Come on, babe, let's go watch the sunrise."

I threw on some clothes and he drove me to Hillsboro Inlet. We sat on the hood of his old blue Land Rover as the sun came up, and he kissed me under a sky of golds and blues threaded with ribbons of pink. We took the picture—with the lighthouse in the background—to mimic the one we'd taken on our first date, my lips pressed against his cheek as he smiled at the camera. I had no idea it would be our last photo.

It's so fucking unfair that Keane is here, and Ben is not. Keane shouldn't be the one sitting in Ben's favorite spot with his hand on the tiller. Tonight he'll be sleeping aboard Ben's boat and there's no fairness in that, either. Keane Sullivan seems like a good person, but he's not Ben, and I can't help wondering if I've made one more mistake. I touch my fingertips to the border of the Polaroid on the wall. *He's here to do a job. He's doesn't have to be my friend. He doesn't have to be anything at all.*

I grab the cans of Coke from the fridge and go back out on deck, but my mood is thrown off.

"Would you mind taking over for a bit?" Keane says.

I'm relieved when he goes belowdecks, but after a bit I hear him rattling around in the galley and catch a whiff of frying fish. He emerges half an hour later with plates of fried mackerel, red beans, and dirty rice.

"I don't expect you to do the cooking," I say. "That's not in the job description."

"Seemed like you needed a bit of space."

"I—Yeah, I did. Thanks for making dinner."

"You're welcome."

We reach the anchorage at Chub Cay at midnight. Together we furl the sails before Keane makes his way up to the bow. He directs me to a large space between two bigger sailboats.

"Now back it up," he says.

I shift the throttle into reverse and watch as he lowers the anchor slowly into the water, letting the boat drift backward until the anchor line grows taut and the hook catches on the bottom. It's a very different method than my throw-and-hope-for-the-best technique in Bimini, when I was lucky the anchor held.

"Next time, in daylight," Keane says, returning to the cockpit and killing the engine, "you should do the anchoring."

I realize now how much Ben used to do when we were sailing together, how often I sat back and let him. Ben might not have been a very skilled sailor, but at least he'd learned how to plot a course and drop an anchor. How naive I was to think I could make this trip alone. "Okay."

Ben is still on my mind as I gather my pajamas, a towel, and my shampoo bar. My skin is sweaty and warm, and my body aches from a long day on the water. I lower the swim ladder over the side of the boat and when Keane goes belowdecks, I shed my clothes as quickly as possible and jump. The initial shock of cool water steals my breath but rinses away the stickiness of the day.

"Anna, are you intentionally overboard?" Keane calls from the cabin.

"Yes."

"Just checking."

He remains below as I climb the first two rungs of the ladder to wash myself. The night air, cool water, and fragrant lemon soap are a sensual combination and my body aches in a different way. I sink back down into the water to rinse, running my fingers through my hair to work out the lather, and down my body, pretending Ben is touching me. It's not the same, but my fingers between my thighs are enough to send a shudder of release through me. Enough that I can climb back into the boat and go down into the cabin.

"Feeling better?" Keane asks, and my face grows warm, as if he knows.

I nod. "Yeah, um—thanks."

"I hope you don't mind, but I've pumped a bit of fresh water to have a wash." He gestures toward the bucket. "Now that you've finished, I'll take a turn in the sea, but I need to bathe my residual limb in fresh water when I finish."

"Totally fine. We have a watermaker."

Keane is wearing his swim trunks as he climbs up into the cockpit, where he arranges his toiletries before he sits to remove his prosthesis. He peels back layer after layer of coverings until he reaches bare skin. His leg ends about mid-calf, tapering to a skinny stump. The solar light hanging in the cockpit is bright enough to see scars crisscrossing the end of his limb like railroad tracks. The skin is pale white compared to the rest of his tanned body.

Keane hoists himself onto the port side of the boat and

pivots on his butt. *"Allons-y,"* he says, giving me a wink before pushing off and dropping into the water.

While he's bathing, I change into pajamas and gather the day's dirty clothes into my laundry bag. Several minutes later Keane is back in the boat. I carry the bucket up to the cockpit, where he has changed out of his swim trunks and into a pair of loose basketball shorts. He rinses the seawater from his limb, then washes out the liner—the layer he wears closest to his skin.

"Salt water can leave behind an abrasive residue," he explains. "With my prosthesis pressing against the stump all day, it's important not to have irritants between the two."

When he's finished, Keane dumps the water and clips the liner and his wet trunks onto the lifeline to dry. He slides along the cockpit bench to the companionway and easily climbs on one leg down to the cabin floor. He's done this before.

I stow the swim ladder and go back down into the cabin. Keane is making up his bed using one of the sleeping bags as a sheet and another as a pillow. I take one of my spare pillows from the V-berth and hand it to him. "Use this."

"I couldn't."

"I have four pillows. Please take it."

"Thank you." He settles back on the quarter berth, resting his dark head against my pillow. I switch off the cabin lights and climb up into my bed. It isn't long before Keane's breathing falls into the steady rhythm of sleep, but I'm wide-awake. The first time I shared a bed with Ben, I couldn't fall asleep. Every place where his body touched mine felt alive and my nerve endings were so lit up, I was awake all night. It's not like that now. Keane

Sullivan is not touching me. And I don't have feelings for him. But I'm not so far away that I can't hear the sleeping bag rustle when he shifts. It feels too close.

The floor creaks as I creep from my bed, comforter and pillow in hand. I climb up to the cockpit and make a new bed for myself on one of the benches. It's not as comfortable as the V-berth, but the air is cool. The space around me feels wide and stars fill the sky. It takes no time at all for me to fall asleep.

off balance (6)

"Was I snoring?" Keane sits opposite me in the cockpit, dressed for the day in a pale blue T-shirt and shorts, his prosthesis in place. I sit up, and he hands me an egg-and-cheese sandwich wrapped in a paper towel.

"Thank you. No," I say. "I couldn't sleep."

"You miss him."

"Ben and I were supposed to take this trip together, and on the day we planned to depart, I just . . . left. But now . . ." I trail off, searching for the right words.

"Now you're on a boat with a strange man who is neither a lover nor a friend, and it doesn't feel right," Keane offers.

"You're very perceptive."

He takes an enormous bite of his sandwich and holds up a finger while he chews. In the sunshine, his eyes are flecked with green and gold. He swallows. "I'm not here to cause you stress,

Anna. If you'd feel more comfortable with me sleeping on deck, I'll do that. I will operate as far in the background as you like."

My eyes sting with tears, thinking about everything he has done for me in such a short time. "Why are you being so nice to me?"

His brows pull together as though the question is preposterous. "Why would I be anything else?"

I take a deep breath to keep the tears away, and nibble a bit of egg sticking out from my sandwich.

"Obviously, your situation is much more painful than mine," Keane says. "But I do understand loss. For what it's worth." Before I can say anything, he stands. "After you've eaten, we can leave. Unless you'd like to go ashore and have a look around."

"I'd rather keep going."

With the sun rising behind me, I finish my sandwich. Keane makes coffee while I brush my teeth, get dressed, and braid my hair. Together we stow away our bedding and make the cabin secure for sailing.

"The wind will be on the nose today, so it could get a bit bumpy," he says. "We can motor or attempt to sail."

"Let's sail."

"That's my girl." The words are barely past his mouth when his neck goes red. "Just, um—a figure of speech." He clears his throat. "I'll get the anchor, shall I?"

In a matter of minutes, we pass from green water so clear you can see a bottom freckled with swimming fish and starfish as big as dinner plates, into a blue so deep it seems bottomless. Into the Tongue of the Ocean, a trench that stretches down more than a mile. The picture I snap of Chub Cay fading behind us is beautiful, but the reproduced color can't even come close to the original.

"Does it ever get old?" I wonder aloud. "I mean, I can't imagine growing tired of this blue, or the green around the islands. It's so peaceful."

"I reckon if you stay in one place too long, you might start taking it for granted," Keane says. "But if you keep moving, everything holds its wonder. At least that's been my experience."

In this regard, he reminds me of Ben. Ever moving. Never waiting for trees to spring up and block the view of the forest. I feel a catch in my chest, but I breathe through it, not wanting to cry in front of Keane again. Or at all. Instead I think about what lies ahead. Nassau was never part of the original plan. It's not on the map. But since the moment he stepped onto the boat, Keane has been keeping a running list of things I failed to bring— jack lines, radar reflector, a lock for the dinghy. We need to stop for supplies.

"Have you been to Nassau?"

"Once," Keane says. "It's a busier place than Bimini with the cruise ships coming and going. A bit less rustic. A lot more tourists. But we should be able to get everything we need."

"I don't want to stay long."

"Understood," he says. Then: "Do you come from a large family, Anna?"

"I have a mother, an older sister, and a niece who is two." I explain how I haven't seen my father since he left, that he has a whole new family. "What about you?"

"Oh, my family is one large Irish Catholic stereotype," he says. "My parents are married near on fifty years and I'm the last of seven. My mom calls me the tiebreaker, since I have three sisters"—he pronounces it *tree* instead of *three*—"and three brothers. Which meant someone was always threatening to belt me if I didn't take their side."

"It sounds fun, though."

His smile is luminous. "Oh aye, it is."

"Do you see them often?"

"Usually at Christmas," Keane says. "My da owns a pub, so all the family comes from far afield—brothers, sisters, and I think we're up to about a dozen nieces and nephews—and we gather at the pub to celebrate. It's my favorite time of year."

"I bet you're the cool uncle, huh?"

He laughs and spreads his arms wide, as if the answer should be obvious. "The older ones have convinced the littles that I'm a superhero. Keeps them from being bashful about the leg."

"That's sweet."

The wind freshens and waves start breaking across the bow, spraying us with a fine mist that thickens my hair and salts my lips. We pull on our foul-weather jackets.

"I reckon we ought to reef the main," Keane says. "Do you know how?"

"No."

"Take the tiller. As soon as I'm on deck, head to wind."

He scrambles on top of the cabin as the boat pounds through the waves, and I don't know if I should be worried. He's wearing sailing sneakers with good traction and bracing himself against the mast, but I can't help wondering how his balance is affected. Yet as he lowers the mainsail a couple of feet, creating a smaller surface area, Keane is as off balance as anyone would be in a sloppy sea, and the same kind of careful coming back down into the cockpit.

"You needn't worry about me."

"Actually, I was still trying to decide if it would be worth the effort," I say, eliciting a small laugh from him. Keane laughs often. Not that Ben didn't, but there were days when he wouldn't get out of bed. He would hardly speak, let alone laugh. Those were hard days because I wanted to crawl into bed and hold him until he felt better, but I also wanted to get away from him. Like his darkness might be contagious. I should have spent more days in bed with him. I should have tried harder to help him stay alive.

"I already know how the body responds to certain situations on a sailboat," Keane says, pulling me back to real life. He takes over the helm and I sit beside him on the high side of the boat. Nassau is still too far in the distance to see, which makes it feel as if we're sailing to nowhere. "I've learned to adapt. I have to be more mindful than I was before, but I'm disabled, not incapable."

"Well, when it's my turn to reef the sail, I hope you'll worry about me, because of the two of us, I'm most likely to fall overboard."

"If that happens, I'll save you." He nudges his elbow against mine. "But let's add reefing the main and man-overboard drills to the list of things you should learn."

We slog through the bumpy chop for several miles before Keane pulls the plug on sailing. "We're wasting daylight now. Best we motor the rest of the way."

He lowers the main while I roll up the jib. The ride remains rough and the waves still break over the bow, but with the engine running, we make better time. We share a bag of plantain chips

Keane finds in the pocket of his jacket and watch as sportfishing boats and mega-yachts speed past us at varying distances.

It's past noon when Keane makes a radio call to one of the marinas in Nassau to arrange for a dock. "I'm not keen on rowing groceries and supplies out to the anchorage," he says. "And leaving an unlocked dinghy at a landing is a bit like leaving the keys in your car and expecting it to be there when you return."

Despite my worries about how much it will cost, I look forward to being able to step off the boat and use a proper bathroom. Maybe even eat in a restaurant.

His next call, a few miles later, is to Nassau Harbor Control, requesting permission to enter the harbor and informing them we have a dock reservation for one night. That we've come from Bimini. The coral-pink towers of the Atlantis resort are visible in the valleys between waves. As we get closer, the wind begins to calm and the shoreline of Paradise Island emerges, white sand and green vegetation. We peel off our jackets, the boat passing from the Tongue back into shallow turquoise water, where schools of silver fish flash in the sunshine.

Between Paradise Island and New Providence, Nassau Harbor is filled with boats of every size and variety, including five cruise ships that mean the nearby streets will be busy with tourists. We skirt the cruise docks and pass under the two bridges that connect the islands before reaching the marina. Keane hands over the tiller and prepares the lines, while I bring the boat alongside the dock. I'm too far away—afraid of a repeat performance of Miami—but he tosses a line around the piling and pulls us close.

stinging mark (7)

Nassau is every bit as disappointing as it is familiar. Aside from driving down the left-hand side of the road, it's a lot like Florida. The main shopping drag is lined with the same types of tourist shops, chain restaurants, and upscale retailers as Key West. Ten bucks will get you three cheap T-shirts, exactly like the beach shops back home in Fort Lauderdale. There's a Starbucks. Burger King. KFC. And with all the pale Americans flooding the sidewalks, it sounds like we're in the United States too. I understand why Ben didn't want to come here. There's nothing wrong with Nassau, but there's nothing really special about it either.

Our first stop the following morning is the marine supply store for the items on Keane's list, along with a heavier anchor, extra propane for the stove, and a canvas tarp to tent across the boom to provide shade when we're at anchor. Ben was going to have a Bimini top installed over the cockpit, but he never did.

We have lunch at a Bahamian restaurant that serves stewed conch with tomatoes and peppers, then take a cab to Nassau's version of Walmart to restock the galley, and as I collect receipts, I worry that I won't have enough money to finish the trip. Ben left a decent amount in our shared bank account, but there are still so many miles, so many islands, between here and Trinidad. So many things that could go wrong. And when it's over, I need to get home.

After everything is unpacked, I head to the marina bathroom to take a shower. I return to find Keane parked in front of a small laptop, a scowl etched into his usually sunny face. He slaps the computer shut without acknowledging my return, grabs his bathing supplies, and stalks off the boat. While he is gone, I break out my own laptop and connect to the marina Wi-Fi to find an email from Carla.

Anna,
A small part of me is pissed that you left town without telling me. We've been best friends this long for
a reason. I mean, you can trust me with your shit. But
a bigger part of me is happy that you finally stepped
back into the world. Be brave but careful. Be smart
but also reckless once in a while. If you have sex with a
stranger, use protection. And don't sink the boat.
Love,
Carla

I send back a brief reply, letting her know I'm in Nassau and that I've hired a guide. Someday I'll tell her how I met Keane

Sullivan, but for now it's just too weird. I'm about to email my mom when I get a message from Rachel.

Did you steal that boat?

What?! No!
Ben left it to me.

His mother has been trying to
contact you. Because she's
contesting Ben's will,
she says you've technically
stolen the boat. She's giving you
the chance to return it before they
get their lawyer involved.

That's not right.
My name is on the title.

Do you have proof?

Yes.

Scan it and send it to Mom.

Okay. How's she doing?

I'm surprised you care.

Don't start.

Just send proof you own the boat.

I frown, waiting for her to say something else, but she's gone.

Keane hasn't returned, so I leave a note that I'm running an errand, and hide the hatch key under the buffing sponge inside an old Turtle Wax tin. The tin is nearly as old as the boat and it's one of those products that's so common, no one would even think to look for keys inside. Still, I'm a little nervous and consider waiting for Keane, but I need to find an internet café before it gets too late.

The café is a short walk from the marina. I scan the title, attach it to an email to my mother, and return within half an hour. Keane's red towel hangs over the lifeline, but he's nowhere to be found. When I think about our afternoon in Nassau, I can't pinpoint anything I might have done wrong. I bought everything on his list without complaint and spent more money than I'd intended. Something—or someone—on his computer must have set him off.

I watch a movie on my laptop while I wait for him to come back. Fix a salad for dinner with some lettuce that's starting to go brown and the leftover fried mackerel. Make up Keane's bed and mine. Try not to worry about someone I have no business worrying about. All around me, Nassau is wide-awake and pulsing with energy. People are laughing and talking throughout the marina. Even when darkness falls, boats motor up and down the channel. I distract myself with a book until my eyes get too heavy to stay open.

A boat-shaking thump jolts me awake, my heart hammering in my chest and my brain automatically assuming a boat thief or worse.

"Fuck." The word is loud, clear, and Keane. I let out a shaky breath and climb up into the cockpit, hoping he hasn't woken up the entire marina. I find him sitting on the floor, rubbing the back of his disheveled head.

"Are you okay?"

"Fuck." He mutters it this time. "I didn't mean to wake you. Had a bit of a crash landing, is all. Anna—"

"Are you drunk?"

"Aye, but, Anna—"

The alcohol fumes rolling off him are strong enough to light on fire. "Exactly how much did you drink?"

"Only four shots of Jameson." He holds up two fingers and squints one eye, making me wonder if he's so drunk, he's seeing double. His accent is deeper, more Irish than usual. "But I lost count of the pints somewhere after eight."

"Eight beers? Why aren't you dead?"

"I'll surely be asking myself the same in the morning, but, Anna, listen," he says, his voice serious. "There's something I need to tell you. It's of critical importance."

"What?"

"Swimming with the pigs is a terrible plan."

The next destination in Ben's chart book is Big Major Cay, an island in the Exumas inhabited only by wild pigs. Ben and I had loved watching videos of people swimming with the pigs and camping overnight on the beach. At the grocery store, I told Keane I wanted to go to Pig Beach. He'd simply nodded and grabbed a sack of potatoes so we'd have something to feed them. So I'm confused—and a little pissed off. "No, it's not."

"It is, Anna." Keane lies back on the cockpit floor as if too drunk to stay upright. "They may well be fucking adorable with their wee snouts"—he gestures above his nose—"but they'll eat all your spuds and want nothing more to do with you."

"It doesn't matter." I'm more than a little pissed off now. "This is something Ben wanted to do, so we're doing it."

"Well, Ben was stupid," he says. "Stupid for wasting his time on bloody fucking pigs and stupid for leaving you behind."

His words leave a stinging mark on my heart, the way skin feels after it's been slapped. I wait for him to apologize, or to say anything at all, but the silence is punctuated by the drunken snore of a sleeping man. The better person inside me wants to remove his prosthesis so his skin won't get irritated, but I'm not the better person tonight. Keane Sullivan can go to hell.

I leave him lying in the cockpit and wonder if he thinks this whole trip is one big joke. If he's humoring the silly runaway American girl to get himself a free trip to Puerto Rico. Except my thoughts catch on the last part of what Keane said—about Ben being stupid for leaving me behind—and I wonder what, exactly, he meant.

* * *

Keane sits up, groaning and blinking in the sunlight, as I step out on deck with my morning coffee and a bagel. He runs his hand over the back of his head. "Jesus." He pulls his fingers away, examines them as if expecting blood, and looks up at me. "How big an apology do I owe you?"

"What makes you think you owe me one?"

"Because you're looking at me as if you've found me stuck to the bottom of your shoe," he says. "And if I didn't, you'd probably have brought me a cup of coffee too."

"Maybe even a bagel."

"Ouch. What exactly did I say?"

"That swimming with the pigs is a terrible idea."

He takes a deep breath and blows it out slowly. "Well, to be truthful, it's turned into a bit of a tourist trap, but I should have kept that opinion to myself. It's not my place to question your decisions. You're the boss."

"You also said Ben—" I stop. Putting Keane on the spot will be embarrassing at best. At worst, he'll be forced to admit something he might never have said while sober—something I don't want to confront. "You said Ben was stupid for wanting to waste his time on pigs."

"Christ." He tips backward until he's lying on the deck again. "I'm a useless bastard and you should probably put me off the boat immediately. I am so sorry, Anna. I reacted badly to some disappointing news and it was wrong of me to take it out on you. Can you forgive me?"

"We're going to Pig Beach."

"Yes, we are."

"You should probably clean up," I say as he slowly gets to his feet. "You've been wearing your leg all night."

Keane returns from the shower dressed in an olive-green T-shirt and a pair of khaki shorts. He smells like sunscreen instead of whiskey. "I have one more errand before we go," he says, dropping off his toiletry kit and a different prosthetic leg that has a web of white plastic. The socket is blue with a raindrop pattern that suggests this is some sort of waterproof leg. "Shouldn't be more than fifteen or twenty minutes."

True to his word, he's back on time and carrying a small outboard motor on his shoulder. Just about the right size for a din-ghy. "I'll have to build a bracket for it"—he holds up a plastic shopping bag—"but now we won't have to row."

An outboard for the dinghy was another thing Ben never got around to buying. He could have afforded a brand-new motor, but one of his favorite games had been finding deals online, so I know how much outboards cost. "I can't—I don't have the money for that."

"I know a guy," Keane says. "And this one was a steal because it doesn't run. Yet."

I try not to smile, but I can't help myself. It's a thoughtful ges-ture and, although I don't know him well, buying a broken engine as an apology seems like a very Keane Sullivan thing to do. "Are you sure you can fix it?"

He shrugs. "About eighty-two percent."

A laugh escapes me. I can probably forgive him. "Thank you."

"No, Anna, thank you."

"Shut up," I say. "Let's get out of here."

a small fire (8)

Nassau at our backs, the Alberg finds a six-knot groove and soars toward the Exumas. We return to deep water, rich blue and rolling, and the rush of waves along the length of the boat is music. Wind and water come together like a song. Pleasure and guilt weave a vine around my heart when I try to conjure Ben, but there's nothing like this in our history. I will never create another new memory with him.

I escape into the cabin, trying to keep Keane from seeing me cry. I'm wiping my eyes on my T-shirt when I hear him say my name. "Bring the bucket when you come, will you?"

His tone is calm, so we're not sinking. I don't think there's any need to panic, but I grab the bucket and quickly climb topside. Something shoots past my head and splashes back into the sea. Scattered around the deck are half a dozen flying fish, in various stages of death. Some of the little silver bodies are unmoving—dead on impact—while others heave, their gossamer wings spreading and fluttering as though trying to take off.

"Scoop them up," Keane says as another fish flings itself into the cockpit. "We can have them for dinner."

Flying fish are not a new phenomenon for me. Ben and I encountered them once, but keeping one was purely accidental. It flew right past us, through the open companionway, and we didn't find it until we got back to the dock. I'm not sentimental about these little kamikazes, so I gather them into the bucket.

"The fillet knife is in my sailing bag," Keane says. "You'll want to gut them before you put them on ice."

"Me?"

"Why not? This is the perfect opportunity to learn. I'll talk you through it."

The bucket wobbles in my hand as the fish flop around inside. They're so much smaller than the mackerel, and I can see myself slicing open a finger. I hold the pail out to him. "Never going to happen. I will happily cook them, but if you want these fish for dinner, you're going to have to clean them yourself."

Keane looks at me. His eyes are hidden behind sunglasses, but the corners of his mouth twitch like he wants to laugh. Finally he grins and accepts the bucket. "Fair enough."

I take over the tiller.

"So, Anna," he says, slicing open the belly of a fish no longer than his hand. He's brutally efficient, yet somehow gentle. "Do you mind my asking how old you are?"

"Twenty-five. You?"

"I'll be thirty at the end of the month. On the thirtieth, in fact."

"My mom always called those magic birthdays. When your age is the same as the date," I say. "Mine happened when I was five."

"And was it magic?"

"Well, I got everything I wished for," I say. "My grandma made me a cake with purple roses, I got a princess doll with a light-up tiara, and my dad took the training wheels off my bike. It seemed magical at the time, but in retrospect, my expectations were pretty typical for a five-year-old."

"On the other hand, you've had twenty years of believing that certain birthdays hold magic," he says, and a beat later: "I'd wish to be twenty-five again."

There's a note of something in his voice that keeps me from asking why. He does nothing to fill the uncomfortable silence as he finishes the fish. Even after he comes back from putting them on ice, Keane sits in the cockpit, staring off toward the horizon. We sail this way for miles, running along the Exumas chain, until it looks like the sun is touching the ocean. If the red sky in Bimini was the work of an angry artist, this one is messy purple fingers dragged slowly through gold.

"Christ," Keane finally mutters. "Aren't we a gloomy pair? You, missing your Ben, and me, all maudlin over the shite hand I've been dealt. Then this sky happens, and I think it must be God asking me how I dare wallow in self-pity when he's giving me this gift."

"You still believe in God?"

He shrugs. "Of course. Don't you?"

"He hasn't done me any favors lately."

"I can see how you might feel that way," Keane says. "But

moments like these remind me how much worse my life could have turned out."

"Worse than losing your leg?"

"Aye," he says. "I could have been the guy who did this to me."

I want to know what happened, but I don't want to pry, and Keane doesn't elaborate. Instead he stands. "Think I'll go fry that fish. Hungry?"

"I told you I would make dinner."

"I'm feeling restless."

He leaves me on deck as night settles and stars populate the sky. Pans rattle and Keane whistles a nameless tune while he cooks. Ben and I never got comfortable using the stove when we were underway. The pitch and yaw of the boat made conditions too unpredictable. We almost always brought picnic foods so we could avoid cooking. But Keane seems unbothered by the wind and waves. It's maybe an hour later when he brings up a citronella candle and what's left of the bottle of wine I opened in Bimini, then returns with plates of flying fish with steamed potatoes and cabbage.

He takes the helm and I fork off a bit of fish. The outside is crisp, while the inside is delicate, not fishy at all. "This is better than anything I could have made," I say. "I'm feeling pretty spoiled."

"Remember it with fondness," he says. "Because when we're making the passage from the Turks and Caicos to San Juan with no land in sight and the possibility of eight-to-ten-foot swells, you'll be wishing for something other than instant soup and noodles."

"Seriously?"

"It can get ugly."

"God, I would never have been able to do that by myself," I say. "I barely made it from Miami to Bimini."

"But you made it." Keane takes a drink from the wine bottle and offers it to me. Putting my lips where his have been seems too personal, but I push the thought aside. It's only wine. "Even I wouldn't want to do a solo passage to San Juan, though."

"Do you think I'll be able to sail the Caribbean by myself?"

"Absolutely," he says. "You'll be island hopping again, so you'll make good time unless you run into bad weather. Since it's nearly winter, there's always a chance of that."

"What should I do if there's bad weather?"

"If you're sailing, keep going," he says. "But if you can wait it out, stay where you are and drink a little more rum until the weather improves. It always does."

We polish off the fish and as I'm finishing the dishes, Keane calls down that it's time to make the tack that will take us to Pig Beach. It's dark, so I won't be able to visit the beach until morning, but a rush of excitement bubbles up inside me as I think about fulfilling one of Ben's goals—and seeing the pigs for myself. I go out on deck and we make the tack.

With the boat on course, we finish the bottle of wine, passing it back and forth. By the time we reach the island, the alcohol has banked a small fire in my belly that's warm and content. In Bimini, I was drunk and out of control, but tonight I enjoy the peace.

We are not the only boat in the anchorage. More than a dozen others dot the crescent-shaped bay when I scramble up to the bow to lower the anchor. It's late, so most of the boats are dark, their anchor lights like extra stars.

"Do you want to go for a swim?" I strip down to my bikini and step over the stern rail.

"From one to Bimini, how drunk are you?" Keane asks.

I laugh. "About a three."

"I'll be right in."

I dive off the boat into the water, where I float on my back, looking up at comets streaking across the night sky and trying not to wish for Ben. From the corner of my eye, I can see Keane, floating beside me. We stay that way for a long time, not speaking. Not even when a tear trickles from the corner of my eye into the ocean.

My fingers are pruned when we climb back onto the boat. I go below and fill the bucket with water for Keane's residual limb, then change into my pajamas. I'm already in bed when he comes down into the cabin.

"Thank you for bringing me here," I say. "Especially when you're not thrilled with the plan."

"I'm fine with the plan," he says. "I just hope it lives up to your expectations."

* * *

Ben was wildly excited about the pigs. Some stories say they were left by sailors intending to return to eat them. Others say the pigs swam ashore after a shipwreck. Either way, they escaped domestication, and I think that's what appealed most to Ben. He went to Princeton, studied business, and went to work at his family's logistics company to live up to his parents' expectations. I was an aberration. His mother *hated* that he fell in love with a girl who worked in a tits-and-ass restaurant. I was too blond, too pretty, and too common for a wealthy young man with a Future. Sometimes I wonder if our relationship would have survived his family's expectations. Sometimes I wonder if he killed himself to be free.

As I row to shore with my five-pound bag of potatoes, there are already people on the beach. Some came by powerboat this morning, anchoring in the shallows. Others came by dinghy from boats in the harbor. A small tour boat arrived about fifteen minutes ago with some people from a resort on a nearby island. People seem to be having fun, taking selfies and shooting videos of the pigs. Maybe Keane is wrong.

I reach shallow water and a large brown-spotted sow places a hoof on the side of the dinghy, bellowing at me as she tries to scramble up. Overwhelmed and a little frightened, I toss a potato and she retreats to gobble it down, crunching through the skin and the raw white flesh. Some of the other pigs see this new source of food, paddle over, and swarm me. It takes no time at all to empty the bag.

The food exhausted, the pigs abandon me, swimming off in search of someone else to feed them, the way Keane predicted. I want to cry. Not because he was right. Not because the pigs aren't adorable. But because Ben was wrong. There is no real freedom here. Only an illusion built with rotting fruit, bits of bread, and five-pound bags of potatoes.

I left Keane sitting in the cockpit, clanking and swearing over the outboard motor, adding and subtracting parts in an effort to get it running. I'm not ready to go back yet, not quite prepared to admit he told me so. I drag the dinghy up onto the sand and walk the tide line, gathering stranded starfish. Splashing the living, keeping the dead. Someone at his funeral told me that Ben will always be alive in my memories, but it's not the fucking same at all.

The morning sun arcs upward on its path toward noon and a lizard of unknown origin scurries past my feet when I return to the dinghy. The pigs don't bother me as I row back out to the Alberg.

"Doing okay there, Anna?" Keane asks as I come up the swim ladder. The outboard has been cleared away and I wonder if he's managed to fix it, or if all those fucks were sworn in vain.

"I don't know."

He spreads his arms. "Need a hug?"

I laugh and cry as I step into his embrace. Into arms that know exactly how tight I need to be squeezed, against a warm shirt the smells like salt and engine grease and comfort.

"On another day I might have loved the pigs," I tell his shoulder. "But today . . . you were right."

"I didn't want to be."

"Can we leave?"

"Absolutely. Yes." Keane releases me, and part of me wishes I could have stayed a little longer in the shelter his arms provided. "Whatever you want."

amplified (9)

Port Howe, at the southern end of Cat Island, is a welcome reprieve after more than sixty sloppy miles of motor-sailing from Pig Beach. The water is calm, the day barely past sunset, and only one other boat rests at anchor in the bay, a large ketch-rigged sailboat called *Chemineau*. Old-school rock and roll drifts across the water, accompanied by laughter, a faint hint of cigarette smoke, and a female voice that *sha-la-la*s along with Van Morrison.

"Hello!" a big voice booms across the distance, and three sets of arms go up, waving at us. In one of the hands I see the glow of burning ash. This is the first time we've been welcomed into an anchorage.

Keane cups his hands around his mouth and calls back in greeting as I wave. We position the boat close enough to be friendly, but not so close that we run the risk of colliding.

"Come on over!" the big voice calls when our anchor is set.

After spending the past couple of days in a blue funk, I'm

a little sick of myself. And even though being excited about meeting new people has never been my default, I'm ready to get off this boat. Keane swings down into the cabin and rummages through his duffel.

"Will you be coming?" he asks, sniffing and discarding a gray T-shirt.

"Yes."

Both of us are windblown and steeped in sunscreen, but I scrub my face and replace Ben's old white button-down—my unofficial sailing uniform—with a red floral halter top. I leave my feet bare and spritz on perfume to cover the sweat. Keane changes into a pair of jeans and I wonder if he's trying to hide his prosthesis.

"Makes meeting new people a bit less awkward," he says, reading my mind.

"I guess I'm a little surprised. You don't seem self-conscious about it."

"I'm not, but I don't always want it to be the first thing people notice about me." He takes a bottle of Guinness out of his bag. "I'd rather they notice my charming personality and devilishly handsome face."

"What charming personality?"

"So, you admit, then, that I'm devilishly handsome?"

I tilt my head back and squint. "Nope. Not seeing it."

Keane places his hand over his heart. "You've cut me to the quick, Anna."

I laugh. "Come on, honey, let's go meet the new neighbors."

Together we launch the dinghy and I hold the bottle of Guinness while Keane rows us to the other boat. Their main boom and the mizzen boom are strung with Chinese paper lanterns, and the music has switched to Crosby, Stills & Nash. It reminds me of Ben's collection of old vinyl records, locked in a Fort Lauderdale storage unit with the other things his mother took from me. Ben would love rowing over to meet new people on a boat dressed in light. He'd say the whole point of this trip is to experience a bigger world. I miss my small world that revolved around him, but tonight I refuse to let sadness get a foot in the door.

Keane tosses up a line to a large man with a broad neck and hair the same color as moonlight. His skin is tan, his face wide. Everything about him is big. And when he smiles, there's a gap between his front teeth. He looks much older than I am, older than Keane, and he welcomes us aboard *Chemineau* with vigorous, crushing handshakes and an accent that is flat and unfamiliar when he tells us his name is Rohan.

"These are my friends," he says, leading us to the center cockpit, where a woman sits with her arm draped like a cat over the second man's shoulder. Smoke curls from a cigarette between his fingers. Both have dark hair, but his skin is white while hers is dark. "James." Rohan gestures toward the man. "And Sara."

Keane introduces us and presents the Guinness as though it's an expensive bottle of wine. "A modest gift, I know. But I brought it from Ireland on my last visit home, so you can be sure it's the genuine article."

Rohan invites us to sit then disappears inside the cabin. Keane takes a seat opposite James and Sara. I move to sit beside him, but Sara pats the empty space next to her.

"Anna." The neckline of her white peasant top slithers down her arm. Her lips are red, and her black eyeliner is perfect. She looks cool and sophisticated, while I feel like a sweaty milkmaid. I don't look to see if Keane is staring at her, but I'd be surprised if he's not. She's so beautiful that I can barely keep my eyes off her. "Do you dive?"

Ben bought us scuba lessons last year for Christmas, but we hadn't redeemed the gift certificates before he died. "I've snorkeled."

"We'll have to remedy that," she says, as if we're old friends instead of brand-new acquaintances. Her accent is British, which raises her glamour factor by a million. "It's what we do. We dive."

James—all dark eyes and brooding mouth—explains they've spent the past six months exploring the bays and reefs of the Bahamas. Diving caves, swimming with whales, and fishing for lobster. Like Sara, his accent is British. "On paper, Rohan runs dive charters out of Nassau, and we are his crew," James says. "But he takes only enough business to keep us in beer and nitrox."

Rohan returns with icy bottles of Heineken while I'm explaining that Keane and I are sailing from Florida to Puerto Rico, and how I'll be continuing on alone to the Caribbean. It makes me sound far more experienced than I am. I leave Ben out of the story in the same way Keane conceals his prosthesis. I don't want their first reaction to be pity.

As we talk—and James chain-smokes cigarettes—I learn that Rohan's accent is Afrikaans by way of his South African homeland. James is a former professional surfer from Cornwall. And Sara is a British-French-Algerian influencer on Instagram who gets paid to take pictures of herself. Like Keane, all of them are widely traveled, and the deeper they delve into their adventures, the more provincial I feel. Sara reminisces about a dive vacation she took with friends to Pulau Perhentian Kecil, an island I would never be able to locate on a map. James talks about the year he spent teaching English in Japan. And Keane shares a story of doing the Sydney to Hobart regatta aboard a seventy-foot racing yacht. They step on one another's stories where they find common ground, and I'm embarrassed that I've only ever been to the Grand Canyon.

"I've always wanted to see the canyon," Sara offers, and I'm grateful for her kindness. "But that's the thing about America, isn't it? It's so big that it's impossible for Americans to see all of their own country, let alone visit others."

Ben would fit in so much better than I do. His family was wealthy enough to travel the world, and Ben went solo backpacking through Central and South America when he was in college. He would have adventures to share, while I have squabbles with my sister in the back seat of the family car.

After a couple of beers, I excuse myself to use the bathroom. Compared to the Alberg, *Chemineau* is huge and, despite a mess of dive gear and discarded clothing, very well equipped. The V-berth has a bed big enough for someone Rohan's size, and the galley is like a proper kitchen, with a microwave and a washer/dryer combination. When I come out of the bathroom, Sara is waiting beside the door.

"So, Keane," she says. "Is he yours?"

"What?" The question catches me off guard.

"I've been trying to work out whether the two of you are in a relationship."

"Oh. No," I say. "We're just traveling together."

Sara smiles. "He's a bit of a dish I'd like to sample."

In my head, Keane is the man who saved my ass in the most literal sense, but seeing him through her lens brings him into sharper focus. God, how did I not *see* him? "Yeah, I guess he . . . is."

Her laugh is low and smoky. "Did you only now realize?"

"No. I mean . . . maybe?"

Her perfect eyebrows arch. "Does this change your answer?"

I don't want to lay claim to Keane Sullivan, but suddenly I feel a fierce protectiveness when I think about his leg. Will Sara feel the same when she finds out? Or will she see him as flawed? "No. He's not mine."

Back on deck, it's as though Keane has been amplified and I notice everything. How his smile always looks like he's on the brink of laughter. The expansiveness of his gestures when he talks, as if the whole world is invited to his personal party. And his shoulders are . . . perfect. Looking at him is like looking at a bare light bulb and when I close my eyes, I can still see his outline.

Sara doesn't take up her old space beside James. Instead she moves closer to Keane, and it swirls up a storm of unease in me. Not jealousy, but a sense that she had better be worthy of him. And I feel ridiculous because their affair is none of my business.

It is past midnight when James stubs out his last cigarette and unfolds from the seat and waves. "I'm calling it a night. Pleasure meeting you both."

"Where are you headed next?" Rohan asks me. Sara touches Keane's arm and laughs. He's telling her a story about another sailboat race, and her smile, her undivided attention, has made him angle his body toward hers.

"We're hopping our way toward the Turks and Caicos," I say. "Rum Cay tomorrow, then Samana and Mayaguana."

Rohan takes a long swig of beer. "We're going ashore at Port Howe in the morning," he says. "Perhaps you could join us, and we can travel together to Rum Cay the following day."

"I love that idea," Sara says, interrupting Keane. "Anna, you and I could sail together on your boat. Leave these boys behind."

"What do you think?" I ask Keane, trying to telegraph my concern that Cat Island is not a part of Ben's plan. But Keane doesn't pick up my signals, and says, "Sounds grand."

"Then we have a date." Rohan says it like an official proclamation. He stands and begins gathering the empty green bottles that litter the table. His arms full, he wishes us a good night and heads off into the cabin. We are down to three and one of us does not belong.

"I think I'll head back to the boat. If you, um—" I stop, not wanting to sound like I expect them to fall into bed together the moment I leave, even though I'm pretty sure that will happen. "I can come back in the—"

"No sense in that," Keane says. "I'm ready to go."

If Sara is disappointed, she disguises it with good manners, kissing us on both cheeks and telling us how happy she is to meet us. "Anna, seriously. The two of us sailing. Consider it. And call over in the morning if you want to go ashore with us."

"We will."

Keane leans toward her, and whispers something that makes her lips curl into a sly, sexy smile, and we leave.

"Nice crowd," he says as we row the short distance between

boats. He faces *Chemineau* and I wonder if Sara is still standing on deck, if he is looking at her.

"Yeah."

"Everything okay?"

I nod, but the truth is, I'm not sure. Now that I've seen Keane in a different light, I can't go back to seeing him any other way. He is a man—an exceptionally good-looking man—and we are together on a small boat. The thought makes me nervous in a way it didn't before. "Long day. A little too much beer. But it was fun."

"Do you want to stay another day?"

"I don't know."

"Whatever you want, Anna, is what I want," he says. "But for what it's worth, there are sights on the island you might like to see, including a plantation in ruin and a beautiful abandoned monastery."

Even though this island is not on Ben's route, I would like to see it. "Okay, let's stay."

ghosts (10)

Keane is wearing jeans again when we climb down the swim ladder into Rohan's inflatable, and Sara shifts to make room for him. They smile at each other first, like the rest of us aren't there.

"Good morning!" Rohan booms in a voice too loud for such an early hour. "Sleep well?"

My dreams were about Ben, leaning forward to whisper something in Sara's ear. About Ben sailing off with her, leaving me on a beach full of pigs, desperately flailing my arms and going hoarse from screaming for him to come back. I woke up crying and my throat hurt, as if I'd really been screaming. But out in his bunk, Keane was sleeping soundly. I crept up on deck and finished the night wrapped in my comforter, waiting for my racing heart and shaking limbs to realize it was only a dream.

"Yeah," I lie. "Thanks."

It's a short trip to shore and we drag the dinghy onto the beach near the Deveaux mansion. Keane explains the property was deeded to Andrew Deveaux to use as a cotton plantation, a reward for his role in resisting the Spanish at Nassau in the 1780s. Most of the house is still standing, including a few thick roof timbers, but the inside is a hollow shell, littered with plaster and old wood. James kicks through the rubble, a burning cigarette in hand, while Rohan uses an expensive camera to take photos of a tree that has grown through the wall. Every window facing the bay has a gorgeous view and I lean in the open door frame, looking at the blue-green water and the pretty blue boat that brought me here.

"Some of the islanders believe the spirits of those who once lived in a house remain among the ruins." Keane moves up beside me. "They'll build new houses beside the ruined ones so as not to anger the spirits. It's a lovely way to live, don't you think? Letting the present peacefully coexist alongside the past."

He steps from the doorway and heads toward the beach, where Sara lies on a towel in the sun. He sits down beside her and trickles a bit of sand on her bare stomach until she lifts her head to look at him. I turn away and move on to the kitchen house, where the bricks of the hearth are exposed, some blackened by cooking fires, others green with moss. If there are spirits here, I doubt they are any happier than when they were alive, with fortunes built on their backs and at the tips of fingers bloodied from picking cotton. I feel haunted, but I'm not entirely sure I haven't brought my own ghosts.

Rohan comes to snap photos of the kitchen house remains. "I could use a drink." He drags a hand through the sweat beaded across his forehead. "There's a bar at the resort just up the highway."

"Oi!" James shouts toward the beach, where Keane is patting his prosthetic shin through the fabric of his jeans. He must be telling Sara about his leg. "Drinks!"

Keane helps Sara to her feet, and they walk together toward us, his arms going every which way as he talks, and her smile hasn't diminished. Maybe she's worthy of him after all.

"She fancies him rotten," James says, and I'm about to say that the feeling seems mutual when he continues. "For today, that is. She'll lose interest by morning."

Rohan nods. "She always does."

Keane and Sara reach us, and Rohan—already tired of being on land—fills them in on his plan to spend the rest of the day drinking rum. James and Sara quickly jump aboard this new plan, but Keane looks less than enthused and I'm not about to start drinking rum at ten thirty in the morning.

"I'd like to hike up to the Hermitage." Keane turns to me. "You'll come with me, won't you, Anna?"

"Sure."

We walk along a "highway" of crushed shells—a one-lane road with no traffic—to a small resort. It's not fancy. Simply a row of bright yellow beachfront rooms, sandy grounds, and beautiful flowering trees. The three divers head immediately to the bar, while Keane borrows the front desk telephone to call a taxi service.

We find Sara, James, and Rohan at the honor bar, fixing their own cocktails, and tell them we'll be back in three or four hours. They seem cheered to know they've got that much time to drink.

"I don't know how they can drink so much," I say as Keane

and I backtrack to the highway to wait for our ride. "I mean, you've seen what happens when I've had too much beer."

"You never told me how you ended up in that state."

"I was alone in Bimini and so angry at Ben that I started drinking," I tell him. "And when this guy tried to pick me up at CJ's, I let it happen. We went back to his hotel room and we were about to, um—" The memory of Chris standing naked at the foot of the bed flashes through my mind and my face grows warm with embarrassment. "His wife called—I didn't know he was married—and I bolted. Obviously, I left a couple of things behind."

I expect Keane to laugh, but he looks disgusted, and I hope he doesn't think less of me. "Jesus, Anna, it's a good thing I didn't know that at the time. I'd have panned his fucking head in."

"Hey." I nudge his elbow with mine. "You took me back to my boat. That was above and beyond the call of duty."

He rakes his fingers through his hair, causing it to stand on end. "Common decency should never be considered above and beyond."

"Well, I guess your mother raised you better than most."

At the mention of his mom, his demeanor softens, and he grins. "Have a care, Anna. I tend to fall for girls who say complimentary things about my mother."

"Oh really? How many girls has that been?"

He winks. "Only one."

For the briefest of moments, I puzzle over whether he's serious, but flirting seems to be Keane Sullivan's default mode, so I laugh. "Do you think that's our taxi?"

Bumping down the road is a solitary silver minivan that has long since lost its shine. "The odds are in our favor."

Our driver is Eulalia, an older Black lady who asks us where we're heading. Keane tells her we'd like to hike up to the Hermitage and asks her opinion about the best place for lunch. "Oh, and is there a Catholic mass tomorrow?"

"Holy Redeemer at eleven," she says. "No priest, so it's liturgy only."

"That's a bit late," he says. "What about the Baptists or the Anglicans? When do they meet?"

"Are you allowed to go to a different church?" I ask. "Switch teams for a day?"

"Well, technically, no, but I reckon the good Lord is happy enough to see his people that he doesn't much concern himself with which pews they're sitting in."

Eulalia laughs until tears leak from the corners of her eyes. It's a good thing there are no other cars in either direction because she's not paying much attention to the road.

"Eulalia is a lovely name," Keane says, ratcheting up the charm, making her beam at him in the rearview mirror.

"My mother says 'twas a prophecy," she says. "Eulalia means 'well-spoken,' and I came out of the womb bursting with things to say."

Keane laughs. "My name was prophetic as well. My mother named me for Saint Christopher, patron saint of travelers. Left home at seventeen and haven't stopped moving since."

"Your name is Christopher?" I ask, reminded of the other Chris, the one I'd rather forget.

"Aye, but no one calls me that but my gran and the priest who baptized me," Keane explains. "I had to have a proper saint's name, but Keane is my mother's family surname. She says she called me Keane 'cos after having seven kids she wasn't keen on having eight."

By the time we reach the settlement at New Bight, Eulalia and Keane are fast friends, and we have been invited for lunch at her house. "An hour at the Hermitage should be enough time and I'll come fetch you," she says. "After lunch I'll take you back to Port Howe."

Keane leans forward between the front seats and presses a kiss to her round brown cheek. "Eulalia, you are a gift. Thank you."

As she drives us up the road to the base of Mount Alvernia, she tells us about Father Jerome, an architect, missionary, and Catholic priest who came to the island as a young man to build churches. He built the Hermitage and lived there alone for the rest of his life, coming down the hill only when called upon to provide food and clothing for those who asked.

The 206-foot climb is short, but steep, and trees along the rocky path provide a bit of cooling shade. Tucked beneath the branches, along the path, are small monuments carved with images of Jesus carrying his cross to crucifixion.

"They're called the stations of the cross," Keane explains. "During Lent, we Catholics typically celebrate the stations with prayer, song, and meditation on the Lord's suffering."

He falls quiet and slowly lags behind. At first I study his face for signs of pain, worried his leg can't handle the climb. Instead I realize he's pausing at each of the stations. When he catches me watching, he does a bashful little shrug-and-grin combo. "You can take the boy out of Ireland . . ."

"It's okay," I say. "It's nice that you have something to believe in."

I walk on ahead, leaving him to his meditation, and I'm winded when I reach the summit. From the top of Mount Alvernia, I can see all of Cat Island—the perpetual green of trees never touched by winter, and the bright white sand. Off to the west, the water is turquoise and powerboats leave white trails in their wake. To the east, the deep blue ocean stretches toward Africa. Down south, the Alberg sits in the bay, surrounded by the silver masts of sailboats. Our little water has gotten crowded.

Up here it's absolutely peaceful. No traffic. No music. No noise but the rustle of the trees and the songs of the birds that inhabit them. I'm about to tell Keane that Ben would love it here, when I realize Ben would not love it. He would have loved Eulalia's lyrical accent and drinking with the divers. He'd have loved talking to Rohan. But Ben loved being in motion, not spending time in silent contemplation. He would have filled up the silence with words. As talkative as Keane Sullivan may be, he knows how to be quiet.

"I love this place," I say. "Thank you for bringing me here."

"Nearly all my best discoveries have been accidental," Keane says. "Sometimes you have to toss the map and fly by the seat of your trousers."

We poke around the buildings, squeezing through narrow doorways and stretching ourselves out on the hard slab of wood that Father Jerome used as a bed.

"I could never be an ascetic." Keane lies on his back, his hand folded on his chest. He has to bend his knees to fit. "As far as I'm concerned, a pint of Guinness, a fluffy duvet, and a warm body pressed up against mine now and again are basic human needs. And, to be perfectly frank, Anna, I covet your duvet."

"Doesn't your religion have rules against coveting your neighbor's duvet?"

He sits up, laughing. "Wouldn't be a sin if you'd share."

"Okay. You can use it whenever I'm not."

"We have a deal."

Eulalia's silver taxi is waiting for us at the bottom of the hill, and she drives us to a small wooden house painted the color of the sky. The grass-and-sand yard are boxed in by a peeling white picket fence, and a yellow dog lies in a hollow of shade beside the front steps. We're met at the door by the scent of cooked fish and Eulalia's husband, Robert, a big man with salt-and-pepper hair. She makes introductions and hustles us to her kitchen table, where bits of fried snapper swim in bowls with tomatoes, onions, and chunks of potato.

The rise and fall of Eulalia's voice is like music as she talks about her island, about her sister who runs the bakery, and about her mother's best friend, who climbed the hill every day as housekeeper for Father Jerome. Sitting in Eulalia's kitchen is like being wrapped in the warmest of hugs. It makes me homesick for something I've never really had with my family. Something I'd hoped Ben and I would make together.

"I don't want to leave," I tell Eulalia when we're climbing into her van afterward. "Will you adopt me and let me live here with you?"

She laughs. "I just sent my last boy off to college in Toronto. I don't want no more kids, but you come visit me anytime you like. I'll be here."

The van lumbers back down the road we came from, toward Port Howe, and I watch the island pass by my window. Eulalia sends us off with hugs and kisses, as if we didn't just meet her this morning. Keane tries to pay her cab fare, but she waves him off. "Christmas is coming," she says, meaning families on holiday will make up for our free ride. We give her one last hug, as if that could ever be payment enough.

confession (11)

We find the divers in a huddle on the beach, drunk and giggling, after having gotten kicked out of the resort bar. They are their own tiny universe, but they pull us back into orbit and Rohan ferries us out to *Chemineau*. Sara and Keane make eyes at each other like teenagers, and I'm tired from hiking and stuffing myself with Eulalia's fish stew. I want to go back to the Alberg, but it feels rude to ask.

"I'm going to have a nap," Rohan says. "Please make yourselves at home. Satellite phone. Wi-Fi. Washer. Whatever you need."

"Actually, I do need to check my email."

James leads me down into the cabin to the navigation station and I use their laptop. There are three emails from my mother—unusual since she rarely uses the computer—all asking why I didn't send the title for the boat. By the third email, she is frantic with worry that Ben's mom is trying to have me arrested for grand theft boat. I resend the original email with the scanned title, then send a note to Carla.

> I spent the morning on Cat Island, visiting a hermit's monastery and having lunch with locals. We'll be hopping to some pretty remote islands on our way to the Turks and Caicos, but I might have a chance to write more when we reach Providenciales. I wish I could tell you I'm better, but Ben is still with me and I'm trying—really trying—to figure out how life works without him.

James is chain-smoking and reading a Henning Mankell mystery when I go back out on deck, while Sara is telling Keane a story about a wild night in Tenerife, another place I'm not sure I could find on a map. He looks at her as if he wishes she were naked. I feel so out of place. I wish I had asked Rohan to drop me at the boat. I pry off my sneakers, strip down to my bikini, and adjust the seat of my bikini bottom. "I'm going for a swim. Bring my clothes when you come back."

Before Keane can answer, I dive into the bay. *Chemineau* is not so far from the Alberg that I can't swim the distance. The water is cool on my skin and by the time I reach the swim ladder, I feel better. Without Keane around, I take a real shower. My hair hasn't been this clean since Nassau and my legs are newly smooth. I clip the wet towels to the lifeline. Take a nap. Make a salad out of cucumbers and tomatoes a day away from going bad. I shake the sand out of my bedding. Watch the sunset. Kill the hours that get lonelier the longer Keane is gone. Only six days sailing with someone and already being alone feels a little . . . weird.

The boat rocks when Keane finally climbs aboard. This time he doesn't crash-land in the cockpit. He creeps in quietly, trying not to wake me. I'm lifting my head from my pillow to say hello, when I catch the scent of alcohol, cigarettes, and Sara's spicy perfume. Instead I pretend to be asleep. I am not jealous—Keane is free to do whatever he likes—but I am sharply reminded that I am not traveling with the man I love. I'm traveling with a stranger.

* * *

Our seventh day at sea begins when I step out on deck and discover *Chemineau* is gone. I look to the south, toward Rum Cay, and see the big boat sailing into the distance. The sun is not far above the horizon. They must have made an early escape, but I'm kind of glad they're gone. I put a pot of coffee on the stove and as it percolates, Keane comes slowly to life. He groans as he shambles past me, hungover and uncomfortable after wearing his prosthesis all night. On deck, he removes his leg and dives into the sea. I leave a bucket of cool water waiting for him when he comes out.

"When did *Chemineau* leave?"

"Must have been before dawn," I say. "It's not even eight."

Keane's sigh sounds almost relieved. "I'm not sorry to see the back of them."

"Oh?"

"Bunch of odd ducks," he says as he washes his leg with fresh water. "I don't imagine Rohan dives while drunk, but he seems to spend a hundred percent of the rest of his time three sheets to the wind. James doesn't appear to do anything but smoke, read, and talk about surfing. And Sara . . . well, never mind about Sara."

"Bagel?"

"That'd be grand, thanks."

He leaves his prosthesis off as he eats and occasionally rubs his left knee, the intact one.

"Are you okay?"

"A wee bit sore today is all," he says. "I was thinking I'd see if I can't get the outboard running this morning so I can ferry myself to shore. I put in a call to Eulalia yesterday and she's sending Robert to fetch me for church. Or, us, if you'd like to join."

"I'll come."

He could have worn shorts to church and no one on this little island would have blinked, but as Keane motors us to shore two hours later, he is clad in his Sunday best. The slim-fitting black pants are a bit wrinkled, but paired with a pale green button-down shirt that pulls out the green in his eyes, it is impossible not to notice how beautiful he is. I can't even look at him for fear he'll be able to see through my sunglasses and read my mind. I don't want him. I don't. But Jesus Christ, he's breathtaking.

"Pretty dress," he says over the rumble of the outboard, eyes hidden behind his aviators.

I'm wearing a golden-yellow wrap dress with a pair of leather flip-flops. Yet I feel like a beach bum compared to Keane. "Thank you."

Robert is waiting for us at the Deveaux mansion. He's less talkative than his wife but navigates better around the potholes. He drops us off at Holy Redeemer Church, a whitewashed stone building that resembles the Hermitage.

"It was built by Father Jerome," Robert says when I mention it.

The inside is also painted white, with hard wooden benches

and windows that capture the sunshine and throw it over us. The congregation, made up of Black and white families, is sparse and Keane chooses a pew near the middle.

I attempt to do what everyone else does. I sit when they sit, stand when they stand. I even kneel when they kneel, but I'm half a beat behind, and I feel like an imposter. My family only attends church on Christmas and Easter, and I'm not exactly on the best terms with God right now anyway. Beside me, Keane is solemn. He knows the proper responses and doesn't mumble his way through the songs. His voice is clear and strong.

I zone out during the deacon's sermon, watching the clouds slide past the windows and thinking about Ben. His family is Presbyterian, but he considered himself an atheist and didn't believe in heaven or hell. As I sit in this beautiful place, with a man whose faith is big enough to ferry him across the bay and up a bumpy road to be here, I wonder if Ben might have been wrong. If he'd been a believer, would God have saved him?

Ben's absence cuts clean through me and a tear slips from the corner of my eye. I catch it with the flutter sleeve of my dress. I take in a deep breath, and Keane reaches over, threading his fingers through mine. His hand feels big and safe, and he doesn't let go until he has to walk up the aisle to receive communion.

The deacon stands at the back of the church after services, bidding the parishioners farewell and saying hello to visitors. Keane lags behind until we're the only two remaining and, after we introduce ourselves, he asks the deacon for a private word. They step out of earshot and I watch Keane talk, his eyes worried and his hands busy. The deacon nods as he listens, then says something as he makes a cross in the air above Keane's forehead, a blessing.

"Confessing your sins?" I tease as Keane rejoins me.

He grins. "I doubt the good deacon has that much time to spare. Not to mention that, since he's not a priest, it wouldn't be official."

Despite the casual way he throws off the question, I suspect he really did make a confession, unofficial or otherwise, but I don't press the subject. It's none of my business.

"Thanks for . . ." I lift my upturned palm to indicate the way he held my hand during the liturgy. "I was thinking about Ben."

"I figured as much," he says as we walk from the church to the taxi van.

"Sometimes I wonder if I'll ever stop thinking about him."

"Don't know why you would," Keane says. "Eventually—and I say this from experience—you'll start building a new house beside the ruins of the old. When you're ready, you'll know."

Back aboard the boat, we change into sailing clothes. Keane pulls the dinghy out of the water and lashes it to the deck for the next leg of the trip, while I close all the hatches and put on some music. There's a lightness to our movements and moods. Maybe it's because Eulalia gave me a healthy dose of home and Keane got laid, but as we motor out of the harbor into deep water, we look at each other and smile.

more than you think (12)

It was Ben's idea to go to Rum Cay. He'd seen YouTube videos of some guys kiteboarding and cliff jumping, and he wanted to do that. And while he would never have admitted it, he liked the idea of visiting an island reputed to be named for a West Indian rum-runner that wrecked off the coast. It was one of the few stops on his route where he planned to rent a cottage so we could have a romantic night off the boat.

The seas have swelled since *Chemineau* snuck out of the bay this morning. What was likely a pleasant sail for them has become a battle for us. The late-afternoon sun is shining, but we are pummeled by the wind, and my hands—even wearing a pair of Keane's old sailing gloves—are sore from fighting the tiller.

"Is it absolutely necessary for us to go there?" He eats cold chili from a can with a fork. "Bite?"

I take the offered lump of meat and beans, wondering if he thinks it's weird that we're sharing a fork. And wondering if he wants to avoid running into Sara. The island is not very big. "Ben really wanted to go there."

"Okay," Keane says. "Do you have any specific plans?"

I've always been a little faint of heart about cliff jumping and I don't have the money to rent a kite board, so I'm not sure what to do on Rum Cay. "Not really."

"Maybe this is where you pitch a tent the way you'd hoped to do on Pig Beach," he suggests. "Flamingo Bay looks secluded. No pigs. No people. Good reefs. I'll even stay on the boat, if you want to be alone."

It's not exactly what Ben would do, but it's a good idea. I love camping. "I'd like that. Thanks."

After Keane has scraped the last of the chili from the can, he takes over at the helm and I go down into the cabin. From below, I toss him a bottle of water before crawling into bed. The rise and fall of the boat through the waves lulls me to sleep.

The sun has gone down when I wake, and the travel clock tells me Keane's turn on watch should have been long over.

"Why didn't you say something?" I ask when I'm on deck.

"This boat is a joy to sail."

"She's been the perfect accomplice to all my bad decisions." I tilt my head back and look up at the white sail against a dark sky. "I don't know what I'm doing."

"If you weren't here right now, what would you be doing instead?"

"Going whole days without showering. Slinging beers. Existing," I say. "Barely."

"In a matter of days, you've solo sailed across the Gulf Stream, dodged a one-nighter with a married man, eaten flying fish, and scaled a mountain. Granted, it was a wee hillock of a mountain, but how many mountains would you have scaled otherwise?"

"None."

"So maybe you know more than you think."

"God, you're like an Irish Mary Poppins with facial hair," I say. "Are you ever pessimistic?"

Keane laughs, shrugging. "Not often, but when I am, I tend to get drunk and fall down. Like in Nassau."

"What happened that night?"

"Prior to the accident, I was quite literally one of the best sailors in the world. Now I'm considered a tragedy and a liability to owners who once tripped over themselves to have me crew aboard their boats." There's a note of bitterness in his voice that I can't miss. "They worry I will fall overboard or hurt myself, something that never crossed their minds when I had two in-tact legs. Every single time, their perception of my disabilities eclipses my capabilities. In Nassau, I was stinging from another rejection."

"Why do you keep trying?"

"I don't want to prove them right," he says. "And . . . I don't know what else to do."

"Is that why you're going to Puerto Rico?"

"Yeah. Heard from a guy who knows a guy who knows an-other guy who said there might be someone looking for crew."

I'm about to apologize when I remember he hates that. "That fucking sucks."

Keane smiles. "Thank you."

"You're welcome." I pick up Ben's chart book and open to Rum Cay, shining the flashlight along our route. He wanted to sail into

Port Nelson, the last remaining settlement on the island, but Keane is heading for Flamingo Bay.

"I've been thinking," he says. "I know you had your heart set on Rum Cay, but we can't navigate the bay in the dark. There are coral heads that make it hazardous to try until daylight. We can change course and do some open-water sailing until sunrise, or we could sail on to Samana. I reckon we'd get there midafternoon and gain back a day on our timeline."

It bothers me that we've deviated so much from Ben's route, but I don't want to risk damaging the boat and the reefs in the dark. Keane's logic is sound.

"Samana is uninhabited," Keane says. "You can snorkel an uncrowded reef, camp under the stars on your very own beach— everything you were going to do on Rum Cay—and be one hop closer to the Turks and Caicos."

As Keane adjusts course, I feel a small pang of regret over not getting to see a place Ben wanted to visit, but I swallow it down. He hands over the tiller and returns with cold sandwiches and a bag of Doritos.

"Even though I can, cooking on a rolling sea is not high on my list of favorite things," he says. "When we reach Samana, maybe we can catch a couple of lobsters and have a proper meal."

The rest of the night we stay faithful to our four-hour schedule and every time I come off watch, I sleep so that when we reach our destination, I won't crash. By morning the wind has subsided and the boat glides easily through the water. Keane comes up on deck, yawning and scratching the back of his head. Rum Cay sinks on the horizon in our wake while Samana rises up in front of us.

"Are you doing okay?" I ask. "You've had your leg on for a long time."

"I took it off a bit while I was sleeping," he says. "So I'm good, but I look forward to having a swim."

The anchorage at Samana is on the south end of the island and inside a formidable reef. We have to approach from the west and navigate our way through a break only forty feet wide, following a coral-riddled path to clear water.

"We've got the incoming tide." Keane consults the chart book. "If we shoot for the middle of the break, we should have enough water below the keel."

"It looks scary."

"Indeed. Ready to drive her in?"

"Me? No. I can't."

He rakes his hand up through his hair. "Look, you're a fine fair-weather sailor, Anna, and you're quite brave for striking out alone. But I'm not always going to be with you. The only way you're going to learn is by doing it."

"What happens if I hit the reef?"

"The same thing that happens if I hit the reef," Keane says. "It's pointless to speculate what might happen. What we need at present is to not let fear rule the day. So I'll go up to the foredeck, where I'll spot for coral heads and guide you in."

a universe that is not listening (13)

The water through the cut is a sloppy crisscross chop and I hold the boat to a painfully slow speed as we motor through a mine-field of coral. I don't want to do this. I have an iron grip on the tiller to keep my hand from shaking. My heart is like a wild bird in my chest, slamming against the cage of my ribs. My eyes are everywhere at once. On the depth sounder, which indicates the water is ten feet deep. On Keane's back as he stands in the bow pulpit. On the dark forest of coral on either side of the boat.

"We're nearly through," he calls down to me. "Nearly clear."

The stillness is cut by the muted underwater scratch of coral against the gelcoat, like tree branches dragged across a window. The boat stutters, and the vibration travels up through my feet, into my body.

"Keep going." Keane's voice is calm, but I'm burning with anger and fear. Every instinct I have tells me to stop the boat to keep it from happening again. From making it worse.

"I told you this was going to happen," I say, pushing the words between gritted teeth. "I told you."

"Easy, Anna," he says. "It's going to be okay. Keep going."

My eyes are blurred with tears as we motor the last few yards into a broad sandy-bottomed clearing. The only reason I know we are in the clear is because Keane tells me. He lowers the anchor, and when he calls back to put the engine in reverse, I do. The anchor catches in the sand and he motions for me to kill the motor, and I do that, too. I steel myself, preparing to scream at him, but before I have the chance, he leaps over the starboard lifeline—prosthesis and all—into the water to survey the damage.

"It's right below the waterline," he calls up to me as I stand in the cockpit, seething. "A bit deep, but it's only a scratch. An easy fix."

"You *asshole*."

"Anna—"

"Ben spent a long time making his boat beautiful," I say. "And it's ruined."

"It's not ruined."

"You could have driven us in. This didn't have to happen."

"I could have," he says. "But it's not Ben's boat, Anna. It's *yours* and you've got to know how to sail it."

"Hiring you as a guide was supposed to be the sensible thing to do!" I shout. "You wouldn't have hit the fucking reef!"

I was looking forward to this anchorage, where I could peel off my clothes and wash away the miles between Cat Island and Samana. I imagined snorkeling and catching spiny lobsters for dinner. Instead anger shimmers off me like a hot road and I want to be as far away from Keane Sullivan as my limited world will allow. Except I have a boat to repair.

"I'm sorry about the scratch." Keane climbs the swim ladder. It's odd to see him wearing his leg, and even though I don't want to be worried about him, I can't help thinking water, especially salt water, is bad for his prosthesis. "And it is only a scratch. But I was not wrong that you need to be able to rely on yourself. However, I may have been wrong to push you when you weren't prepared."

A small snort escapes me. "May have been?"

"If you don't want to learn, what's the point of all this?" he asks. "Why not pack it in and go home?"

"I don't want to go home."

Keane looks beyond me and rubs the heel of his hand against his mouth as if blotting the words he wants to say. "Then take responsibility, Anna. Decide you really want to learn how to sail, so that when I leave you in Puerto Rico, you'll be ready for the Caribbean."

He goes down into the cabin for his tool bag before coming back out on deck. "I need your help to fix the boat. I can't do it alone."

I take the bag. "I want to repair the scratch." It comes out petulant.

We launch the dinghy without the engine, and as I row to the starboard side of the boat, Keane pushes the boom out over the port side and hops up to sit on it. The boat heels over and the jagged scar lifts out of the water. It's nearly a foot long and about an inch wide. Deeper in some places than others, but the fiberglass matte is not exposed. It's not as bad as I expected, but looking at it makes me ache.

Following Keane's instructions, I rub sandpaper over the scratch until the bottom paint is removed. The repair compound resembles a stick of modeling clay that I knead until it's soft. I press it into the scratch, using a putty knife to smooth it out. While the compound dries, I watch a school of blue tangs zigzag beneath the dinghy and my anger starts to fade.

Ten minutes later there is a long gray patch in the navy-blue paint. It's not pretty, but the boat is fixed.

"Do you think it will hold?" I ask when Keane and I are both in the cockpit again.

"It should," he says. "But if it fails, we're in no danger of sinking."

My anger has abated, but a thick fog of tension clouds the air between us. I wonder if Ben and I would be squabbling if we had made this trip together. Would I be sick of him? Except I'm not sick of Keane. I'm irritated. Mostly because, as usual, he is right—about everything.

"I'm going snorkeling."

"I'll, um—" Keane stops short of saying he'll join me, which is smart. I want to be alone. "Have fun."

The reef surrounding the boat is in shallow water, and swimming along the surface puts me closer to undersea life than I've ever been. I'm an arm's length from branches of elkhorn coral, and the fish are so close that I can almost grab them. Hidden in crevices are large grouper, and queen conchs are scattered across the sandy bottom.

Keane cannonballs into the water several yards away from me, first as a mass of bubbles, then as a man swimming—fins strapped to both his intact foot and the foot of his waterproof leg—toward a hollow near the bottom of the reef where a spiny lobster hides. Keane uses a tickle stick to tease the lobster out into the open and a net to scoop it up. He surfaces, before returning to the bottom to catch another. The lobsters are so abundant that he doesn't even need to try. I swim away from him and lose track of time, listening to parrotfish chomp algae from the coral with their human-looking teeth, and watching my shadow send tiny fish behind seaweed fronds, where they hide until I've passed.

Keane is washed, dried, and reading a book in the shade of the boom tarp when I come out of the water. The lobsters are in the dishwashing bucket on the floor of the cockpit, scrabbling against the plastic, crawling over each other in an unsuccessful campaign to escape. Keane puts down the book.

"Hey, um—I'd like to apologize for making you do something you were clearly afraid to do," he says. "I overstepped my bounds and forgot that I am, technically, your employee."

I shake my head. "You were right. I need to learn. I hated you for a few minutes, but I'm over it."

Keane grins. "So I don't need these lobsters as a peace offering?"

"Oh, you still need them."

We load everything into the dinghy—tent, sleeping bags, a couple of lobsters bound in aluminum foil, a bowl of chopped apples and grapes masquerading as fruit salad, and a bottle of rosé—and motor to shore, where we dig a firepit in the sand and pile it with driftwood. We wait for the lobsters, nestled among the burning branches, to roast inside their shells, and we watch the sky turn orange and red, as though it, too, is ablaze. Samana is one of the easternmost islands of the Bahamas, off the beaten path, and we are utterly alone.

"The first time I ever had lobster was with Ben." I peel back the foil in tiny increments to keep from burning my fingers. "His mother throws an annual Fourth of July party with giant steamer pots stuffed with lobster, clams, and shrimp. To me, it was always this incredibly expensive thing my mom would order on the rarest, most fancy occasions, and the people at the party were eating it like it was nothing special."

I pop a piece of meat into my mouth. The lobster is slick with olive oil and tangy with bits of fresh lemon—better than any I've ever tasted.

"See, I come to it from the opposite direction," Keane says. "My uncle Colm was a lobsterman, so in summers, he'd bring us pail after pail of the wee bugs. I was about four or five years old when my da—at what must have been our third lobster supper of the week—cracked open a tail and said, 'What do you reckon the poor folk are doing right now?' And I, who had grown excessively jaded with the experience, muttered, 'Eating bloody lobster again.' The whole table exploded with laughter because we were all thinking it."

I laugh.

"He gave me a right bollocking for cursing, but it's still a running joke whenever someone wonders aloud what the poor folk are doing. Eating bloody lobster again."

"You've led such an interesting life," I say. "Mine has been so . . . average."

"I don't know about that." He sucks the flat of his thumb between his lips to lick off the oil. "Here you are, on your own private beach, eating a crustacean who was minding his own business beneath the reef a few hours ago. Seems to me your interesting life is just starting at a different time than mine."

"My sister called me selfish for doing this."

"Reminds me of my eldest sister, Claire," he says. "Her worldview is a bit myopic, not extending much beyond the Dingle Peninsula. She loves me well enough, but she's of the opinion that sailing is not a proper profession and, apparently, there's a misery-to-fun ratio I'm failing to honor. She views my choices through her lens and has arrived at the conclusion that I'm doing life wrong, rather than considering I have a lens of my own."

My breath catches in my chest when I realize Keane Sullivan is the person Ben was trying to be. He planned an adventure he never intended to take, imagined a life he never intended to live. Instead he sailed out on a tide of pills and tequila. Instead I am taking this trip with the person Ben could have been. Should have been.

Everything about this is wrong.

A broken sound crawls up my throat, pushing at the back of my lips, and I stagger to my feet. "I, um—I need—I'll be back."

"Anna?"

I move away from the fire as quickly as the shifting sand will allow, not answering Keane. Not looking back. Closer to the water's edge, the sand is harder, packed tight beneath my feet and I break into a run. The island is small, and the beach is not infinite, but I run until my lungs burn and the fire is distant. I collapse in the sand and howl.

In fury.

In anguish.

For the man I lost.

For the man he'll never be.

I howl until my throat is raw and my voice is a scratch.

"I hate you." I've said those words to Ben's memory before, but this time I don't let guilt try to snatch them back. "Fuck you for leaving me. Fuck you for dying."

The stages of grief are not linear. They are random and un-predictable, folding back on themselves until you begin mourn-ing all over again. I have bargained with a universe that is not listening. I have cried myself hollow. I have leaned into the belief that I can't live without Ben Braithwaite, but kneeling here in the sand on a beach four hundred miles from home says maybe I can—and that terrifies me.

a place to land (14)

Keane is asleep when I return to our campsite. The fire is a pile of crackling embers and the remains of our lobster fest are gone. I've been away longer than I thought. I crawl into a tent that used to be the right size for two people, but now feels too small.

"Hey," Keane says with a yawn. He shifts his arm to make a space for me beside his body. The rage that had almost burned it- self out flares up, sparking an impulse to throw myself at him. Kiss him. Fuck him. Use him. Not to soothe a lonely little ache, but to slash at Ben's memory. Except it didn't work in Bimini. And it isn't Ben who would have to deal with the fallout. Keane and I would be the ones left with the scars.

"I'm a fucking mess."

"I don't mean anything by it," Keane says. "I just thought you might need a place to land."

So I land, stretching out beside him, my head on his shoul- der, as he holds me. There's something about Keane Sullivan that makes me want to burrow inside his chest and live there, safe and warm, but I'm afraid to move for fear he'll think I want something more from him. I close my eyes, thinking instead how far sound carries. How much did Keane hear? "I'm sorry I left. I—"

"You don't owe me an explanation."

"Will you tell me something?"

"What kind of something?"

"Anything," I say. "Just talk until I fall asleep."

His chest quivers beneath my cheek as he laughs. His shirt is soft, and his fingertips are warm on my arm. "This shouldn't take long at all."

I close my eyes and he begins a story about how his mother picked his confirmation name because she didn't trust him to choose for himself.

"To be fair," he says, "I was heavily under the influence of American rap at the time, so my suggestion of Tupac was not well received."

I'm too tired to laugh, but I smile. "What name did she give you?"

"Aloysius."

"That's pretty awful."

"It is," he agrees. "Killed my career as a rapper before it even—"

"Keane?"

"Yeah?"

"Thank you."

His lips press the top of my head. "Go to sleep, Anna."

My heart rate slows, and I focus on the steady thump of his heart as everything in me quiets. I wake some time later, still tucked against him; my arm wrapped around Keane's torso. I should let go, but I don't.

"Are you awake?" I whisper.

"No."

I laugh as I sit up. Gold gathers along the horizon and the sky is early-morning blue when I unzip the tent screen to watch the sunrise. "Did you sleep at all?"

Keane sits up beside me, shaking his arm and wiggling the life back into his fingers. Sunbeams play in the air around him. "A bit."

"Please tell me I wasn't snoring."

"No," he says. "I just didn't want to move for fear of waking you."

"You stayed up all night because—" I rub my hand over my face and blink back tears. "Could you possibly be any nicer?"

He's silent, and when I sneak a glance from the corner of my eye, his mouth seems to be wrestling with itself. I look away. He clears his throat. "Actually . . . I could."

The tent shrinks even smaller. Three years with Ben did not make me invisible. I recognize attraction when I see it and I understand what Keane meant. I just don't know what to do about it. It's been ten months and—My heart free-falls in my chest as I realize I've lost track.

"I don't know about you," I say, scrambling out of the tent, "but I could use some coffee—and breakfast."

"Breakfast," he echoes. "Right."

Keane and I strike the tent, and as we motor away from the beach in silence, our equilibrium is off.

* * *

When it's time to leave, Keane pulls up the anchor and guides me out of the harbor. I'm still afraid, but I focus solely on the channel in front of me and trust the sound of his voice, altering course only when he calls out an adjustment. We make it through the cut without incident and last night's red sunset proves itself true—it's a gorgeous day for sailing. A downwind sleigh ride that will push us closer to the Turks and Caicos.

"So, what's the plan?" Keane asks, taking first watch at the helm. It's early yet, so I sit with him, Ben's chart book spread across my knees. San Salvador Island is believed to be where Christopher Columbus first set foot in the western hemisphere, but according to Ben's handwritten note in the margin of the map, Mayaguana may have been the actual landing spot. "I guess I can see why Ben might want to go there."

Keane doesn't offer his opinion.

"It seems pretty desolate," I say. "Kind of like Samana."

His mouth pinched into a straight line, Keane only nods.

"Clearly you have something you want to say, so say it."

"Mayaguana is very undeveloped," he says. "And Christopher Columbus? He abused the indigenous peoples, introduced them to any number of lethal diseases, and paved the way for the transatlantic slave trade."

This trip is not going the way I expected. Everything is different. "Are you saying we should go straight to Providenciales?"

"I'm not saying anything. But if I were, that's what I'd be saying."

I set aside the chart book and laugh. "Okay. Fuck Christopher Columbus. We're going to the Turks and Caicos."

"Grab the helm."

I take over the tiller, and he disappears into the cabin, returning with the bag containing the spinnaker, a sail Ben and I never used. On the foredeck, he secures the sail bag to the side rail. As he moves, it's clear Keane has done this hundreds of times—maybe thousands—and it makes me sad that the people who once valued him see his prosthesis as a hindrance. The spinnaker crackles like tissue paper as it goes up, fluttering in the wind, flashing bright primary colors on a field of white.

"Now head dead downwind," Keane says, rolling up the jib and trimming the spinnaker. The belly of the sail fills with air and the boat surges forward. Fast becomes even faster and it feels as though we're flying.

"I won't ask you to do that." He takes over the tiller and I shift so he can sit. "Unless you want to learn."

"I don't know." The fat, colorful sail snaps in the wind, the edges curling in and billowing out. "I might."

The hours stretch out like other crossings we've made, long and slow, despite the boat racing through the sea at seven knots, and we fill the time as best we can. Sailing can be romantic. It can be exciting. But it can also be mind-numbingly dull. I find the deck of cards and we play a few rounds of War. When we tire of cards, I bring up the travel Scrabble board and we argue over whether *banjax* is a real word.

"In Ireland it is," Keane says. "It means to make a mess of things, usually by being incompetent."

"We're not in Ireland."

"Well, we're not in the United States, either, but I reckon if you'd just played a twenty-two-pointer with a triple-word score, you wouldn't be arguing."

"No, I'd be winning."

His shoulders shake as he laughs so hard that I start laughing too. When I finally get my breath back, I say, "I have a question."

"Ask it."

"Do you have a home? I mean, like an apartment somewhere in the world where you keep your stuff?"

"I wasn't joking about traveling with everything I own," he says. "I suppose my permanent address is back in Tralee with my folks, but I'm a vagabond. A *chemineau*, if you will."

"Is *that* what it means?"

He nods. "I looked it up."

"Do you ever get lonely?"

Keane is quiet for a few beats. "Sometimes, especially when I'm at home in Ireland, when I see my siblings with their families. I wonder if I'm missing out." He adjusts the trim on the spinnaker. "But companionship is easy enough to find, especially for a handsome bastard like me." He glances at his watch. "You've still got about an hour before my shift ends."

I don't have anything to do, but I feel like I've been dismissed. I go down into the cabin, grab my comforter from Keane's bunk, and crawl into the V-berth. Once I'm stretched out, the wind and waves send me straight to sleep.

* * *

"Anna." Keane's voice burrows into my sleeping brain. It's time to wake up, but I'm not ready. After a long night of sailing, it feels as if I've only been asleep for a few minutes. "Anna." His voice is low, but there's an urgency that pulls me upright. "Come here. There's something you need to see."

I climb up on deck, expecting dolphins or sea turtles, but we're being followed by a small pod of humpback whales. Keane turns the boat into the wind, bringing us to a stop, and the whales surface a few yards from the boat. A large barnacle-crusted head rises out of the water and pushes air from its blowhole, sending a puff of salty spray over us like a misty rain.

"Oh my God."

The whale holds there, watching us until it sinks below the surface. We scramble to the foredeck and sit on the port rail while the boat drifts. The dark bumpy bodies arc through the water, their stubby dorsal fins appearing and disappearing. The large whale moves closer to the boat, rolling over to reveal its white underside and long pectoral fins.

"I think it's showing off." I don't know why I'm whispering, but there are no other sounds except the splash of their huge bodies, and the moment feels too sacred to disturb.

"I reckon you're right."

"This is"—I push away a tear with the heel of my hand— "this is the most amazing thing I've ever seen."

"I have a mate who lived in Martinique for a time." I appreciate that Keane keeps his voice low too. "A few years back we were hanging out on the beach after doing some surfing when a pod of about four humpbacks happened past. They were breaching and lobtailing—that thing where they slap their tails against the water—and it was a spectacular sight, but nothing like being this close."

Two smaller whales seem to be playing a game of how close they can come to the boat, swimming right below our dangling feet, but the large whale is nowhere to be seen. Suddenly, in the distance, the surface explodes, and the large whale leaps out of the sea. The huge body crashes back into the water, sending an enormous white spray up and out, in every direction. The boat dances on the ripples, but neither of us speaks. I don't even know what to say. We sit in silent awe. And when the whales are gone, we let the boat drift.

"I wish——" I stop myself from saying Ben's name, and feel conflicted about that. I still wish he were here, but this experience is perfect without him. It belongs to us—to Keane and me—and all the wishing in the world can't make Ben part of this. "I wish they'd stayed a little longer."

"We could linger a bit," Keane says. "See if they come back."

I shake my head. "That wouldn't make this any more perfect."

He douses the sagging spinnaker and unfurls the jib as I bring the boat back on course for Providenciales. We're still about four hours from the island, but we're in the home stretch.

"I'm going to have a short sleep," he says. "And after, I'll make breakfast, okay?"

"That would be great. And thank you for not letting me miss the whales."

"Seeing them without you wouldn't have been nearly as good."

the next anna (15)

Providenciales brings a dock and real showers. It brings a break from sailing. Dry land for legs that have forgotten how to walk. I head to the customs office at the marina for a new round of paperwork, and my bank account shrinks as I pay the cruising fee and dockage. When I get back, Keane raises the Turks and Caicos courtesy flag and we collapse. Even though we took turns sleeping on the passage from Samana, we're worn out from two straight days at sea. Keane falls asleep stretched out in the cockpit and we eat ham sandwiches for dinner because neither of us feels like cooking.

The next morning Keane sweeps a small beach's worth of sand from the cabin as I gather our laundry. His clothes feel different, smell different than mine, but I try not to let my brain make an issue out of it when I wash our clothes together.

"Did you just get to Provo?" The other person in the laundry room is an older white woman with frizzy graying red hair and sport sandals. She gives me a friendly smile.

"Yesterday. How can you tell?"

"The big bag of laundry gave it away," she says. "That's the first thing we do when we reach a new port. I'm Corrine."

"Anna."

"My husband, Gordon, and I are on the Island Packet down the way," she says. "It's called *Patience.*" I'm constantly surprised by how quickly cruisers invite you into their personal lives, as if having a sailboat makes you part of a secret society. Or maybe days at sea leave them hungry for human contact. Either way, I'm half-expecting Corrine to hand over her email password before long. "We're from Ontario, Canada."

"I have the Alberg," I tell her, which launches her into a story about her husband's first boat being an Alberg before she wanders off on a tangent about how they were high school sweethearts who married other people but reconnected after their spouses died.

"We married, retired, bought the boat, and now we live aboard full-time," she says as Keane enters the laundry room, his hair damp and spiky, the two days' worth of scruffy beard now shaved back to stubble.

He offers to stay with the wash so I can take a shower. I introduce him to Corrine, who begins her introductory spiel all over. Keane is so much better at this than I. He doesn't just have impeccable manners, he has a genuine interest in other people. Keane is a bonder. The next time Corrine meets someone new, she'll likely have a story about the nice young Irishman she met in Provo.

I slip away unnoticed and head for the shower, where I strip the salt from my body. Samana cracked me open. I left a girl-shaped skin on that midnight beach and as I wipe the fog from the mirror, I see the next Anna revealed. Limbs darkened. Hair streaked white by the sun. Unfamiliar and recognizable at the same time. She looks healthier and, maybe, happier.

I dress in a dusty-pink skirt scattered with white polka dots and a navy-blue tank top. Put on makeup. Rub half of it away. By the time I return to the laundry room, Keane is folding our dry clothes and Corrine is gone.

"Win another member for the Keane Sullivan fan club?" I pick through the pile for my underwear. I can't let him fold the holes and period stains and hanging threads.

He laughs. "We've been invited to dinner tomorrow."

"Of course."

"You look very pretty." He tosses the compliment out, his eyes on the shirt he's folding, but the back of his neck has turned pink. My face gets warm. The whole thing feels like a scene out of a high school dance. His sincerity is so much more potent than his casual charm.

"Thank you."

He clears his throat. "We'll need to hire a taxi to get to town. I'll make the call."

Our marina is on the rocky southern shore of the island, very different from the northern beaches that stretch out like a wide golden welcome to the Atlantic. The resorts and villas are up-scale. Places where celebrities are caught canoodling in the ocean.

Keane and I aren't heading anywhere so glamorous. No in-finity pools or private balconies for us. Our destination is the IGA to stock up on foods that will be easy to prepare on the big crossing if the weather is bad. Cup Noodles and pop-top cans of Chef Boyardee. Cold cuts and canned tuna. Cheese and crackers.

On our way back to the marina, the taxi is stalled in slow-moving traffic when we pass a tiny shop with a couple of Jeeps for rent. Keane flings open his door. "I'm going to hire a Jeep."

Before I can say anything, he bolts from the taxi and traffic moves forward, leaving him behind. I'm unloading the groceries from the trunk when Keane rolls up in a bright yellow topless Jeep. He pays the taxi driver, and hands me the keys to the rental. "Want to take it for a spin?"

"Sure."

"I was thinking I might varnish the teak, so if you'd like to explore the island on your own for a bit . . ." He trails off, rubbing the top of his head and looking slightly uncomfortable.

"Is that a euphemism for masturbation?"

Keane laughs. "It could be, but no. What I'm trying to say is that you shouldn't feel obligated to hang around with me if there's something you'd rather be doing. The teak on the cockpit benches could, in fact, use a coat of varnish and I'm happy to do it."

"Then I guess I'll take you up on the offer."

We unload the groceries, and I tuck my ID and some cash into the pocket of my skirt and tie my hair back in a ponytail. Keane hands me a business card with his cell phone number printed on it. "In case you need bail money."

Having never driven on the left-hand side of the road, I spend the first mile feeling like a head-on collision waiting to happen. When I reach a roundabout, I sit too long, afraid to merge into the circle. The car behind me honks impatiently, then cuts around me. Eventually I work up the nerve and take the exit that leads me to the main highway. I drive until I come to a smaller road that runs along the Atlantic coastline—a more rustic version of A1A back home—and stop when I reach a waterfront restaurant called da Conch Shack.

On the beach, a couple of islanders crack open conchs and the scent of fried fish hangs in the air. The place is packed, inside and out, and a pitcher or two of sunset-pink rum punch anchors nearly every picnic table on the beach.

I grab an unoccupied seat at the end of a small bar and order a beer from a bartender named Leon, feeling a little guilty because Keane would enjoy this place. I feel worse when I realize the first person who came to mind was not Ben. Except Keane has been my constant companion for almost two weeks and it feels strange to be somewhere without him.

As I people-watch, the woman sitting beside me tilts her left hand to admire her wedding ring. She's about my age. A newly-wed. My thumb reflexively grazes the underside of my ring finger to adjust my ring, but it's not there.

My engagement ring was a family heirloom and Ben gave it to me on a random Tuesday night while I was watching TV.

"So, there's this secluded little beach in Trinidad called Scotland Bay," he said from the other end of the couch. He'd almost finished charting the course through the Caribbean and was working on the last map. "And I was thinking that if we can make it through the entire Caribbean without you wanting to murder me . . . maybe we could get married on that beach."

I pretended he was interrupting me, even though I loved the idea of marrying him on a secluded beach on a tropical island. "Yeah, I guess."

"Hey!" He snatched the TV remote from my hand and

replaced it with a small blue velvet box. It was old and some of the velvet at the corners was worn away. "I'm trying to propose to you."

On our first date—the one at the lighthouse—he'd spread a blanket on the sand. As we lay on the ground, looking up at the stars, he'd asked me to marry him. I laughed because I'd known him for three days, but I said yes.

"You already proposed," I reminded him. "I've already accepted."

"Yeah, but now I'm being serious."

"Are you telling me you weren't serious then?" I nudged him with my elbow, then opened the box to find a ring—a sapphire set with a halo of small white diamonds and pale blue aquamarines. My breath rushed out in a soft oh. I hadn't ever imagined the perfect engagement ring, but this was it.

Ben took the ring from the box. Slipped it on my finger. Before he kissed me, he said, "I was serious then. Now. Always."

I look at my bare hand. Ben's parents took the ring after Ben died. It belonged in the Braithwaite family, their lawyer told me, and there was nothing in Ben's will that said otherwise. All that remains is a fading tan line around my finger where the ring used to sit.

Fuck this. I'm not going to sit here feeling terrible. And after ten months of isolating myself from well-meaning friends and family, I'm kind of over being alone. I flag down the bartender.

"Hey, Leon," I say. "I need something fun to do this afternoon. Something off the beaten path. Something adventurous."

"I know just the place." He grabs a paper napkin and talks while he draws a map. "It's called Osprey Rock and it's quite remote, so you need to be careful. Do you have a car?"

"Yes, a Jeep."

"Good. The road is very rough," he says. "Out there is a cove you can explore that pirates used as a hideaway, and if you're feeling brave, you can cliff jump at Split Rock, but I don't recommend doing that alone."

"This is perfect. Thank you."

On my way to the Jeep, I text Keane.

```
What you need: towels, swim trunks, water
leg, lunch food, booze. I'll be there in
about fifteen minutes.
```

already mine (16)

"Anna, you have to tell me where we're going," Keane says as Leon's directions take us down miles of bumpy dirt road, past salt flats and through scrubby vegetation that make it seem like we're hopelessly lost. "What if it's dangerous for a disabled man like me? It's irresponsible for you not to tell me."

He's been trying to pry the secret from me since I got back to the marina and told him we were going somewhere cool. I laugh. "You'll be able to do this. Trust me."

After about five or six miles, when it feels like we are as far from civilization as we can possibly get, we reach a dusty parking lot beside a small beach. I glance over at Keane, who grins. "Oh, this is grand."

"It gets better."

We lock our valuables in the glove compartment and follow the curve of the beach toward the cliff path marked on Leon's napkin map. As we're walking, I notice a small white-and-brown dog sitting on the sand. There's no one else on the beach—not a soul for miles—and I wonder if the dog is lost. It stands, tail wagging as we pass, but doesn't try to follow us.

We hike up a path lined with cacti and other prickly wind-swept foliage that push stubbornly out from the cracks in the rocks, until we reach a series of large holes in the ground, one of which has a wooden ladder extending down into the cliff.

"So, according to my bartender, pirates used this cove as a hideout," I say right as Keane says, "Anna, look at this."

He's pointing at a patch of rock carved with SHIP ST. LOUIS BURNT AT SEA 1842, the first S worn away with time and weather. There are other rocks with the names and dates of people and ships, some as old as the late 1700s. Most of the words have been weathered too smooth to read.

"I wonder if the *Saint Louis* was captured by pirates en route to its destination and was towed here," I say.

"It's possible," Keane says. "Perhaps once they'd plundered the cargo hold, they set fire to the ship. Or it could have blown off course in a storm and got struck by lightning. But these carvings . . . they feel like graffiti. Or pirate bragging rights. This is brilliant."

We climb down the ladder into the cave. The sun is high in the sky, drenching the space with light. The mouth of the cave overlooks a tiny sheltered cove. In the eighteenth and nineteenth centuries, the cave would have blended into the rocky coastline, rendering it practically invisible. I spread a blanket on the floor, where we eat sandwiches and drink Red Stripe. I snap dozens of pictures with my phone before snatching up a driftwood stick from the floor and holding it against Keane's neck, like a sword. "Surrender all your treasure or I'll slit your throat."

He burrows his hand into the pocket of his shorts and produces a one-cent coin with a harp on one side and a Celtic bird on the reverse. "An Irish penny from my birth year," he says, placing it in my palm. "It's traveled the world with me."

"You'd better keep it." I hand him the coin. "It might be good luck."

"You'd make a terrible pirate," Keane says, but returns the penny to his pocket and smiles like he's glad to have it back. "This place is fucking fantastic."

"It gets better."

"You've already said that."

"I know." I poke him lightly between the shoulder blades with the stick. "But back up the ladder you go."

Leaving our clothes in the cave, we climb up to the top of the cliff and follow the scrub trail to the very tip. Separated from the bluff is a column of rock with an osprey nest at the top. We stand at the edge of the cliff. The drop is about fifty feet, straight down into crystalline turquoise water. In the distance a sailboat heads toward Puerto Rico—or maybe the Dominican Republic—and Keane's smile is luminous. "This reminds me of my friend's place on Martinique."

"Want to jump?"

I didn't think it was possible for his smile to get wider, but it does. "Are you sure?"

"No, but . . . yes."

He laughs. "On three?"

"One . . . two . . . three . . ."

The wind rushes past me as I drop, my body straight as a pin. As far as jumps go, it's not terribly daring, but the distance between the cliff and the water feels like forever. My feet slide first into the ocean and the force of impact wedges my bikini bottom into my ass crack. I knife through the water, deep enough that my toes graze the sandy bottom and I feel the depth pressure in my head. I propel myself upward toward a bright spot of sunlight. Keane's treading water beside me when I come up. "How was it?"

"Terrifying and amazing."

He nods. "Thank you for bringing me here, Anna."

"Thanks for coming with me," I say. "Here . . . and on this trip. Maybe I could have done it all by myself, but it's better with company."

We swim until we reach the pirate cove, where we lie on our backs in the sand, watching the puffy white clouds drift past. The sun is warm on my skin and I can't remember the last time I felt so content.

"Can I ask you something?"

"Anything," Keane says.

"What, um—what happened to your leg?"

"I was in Saint Barths for the New Year's Eve Regatta," he says. "It was a fast round-the-island race, just a bit of fun. Nothing serious. We finished in first place and the owner of the boat took the crew out for victory drinks. Outside the bar, I realized it had gone midnight in Ireland, so I paused to ring home and wish the family well. I was standing in the road between two parked cars when a Mercedes came around the corner and struck the first car, pinning me between the bumpers. Broke my left leg. Shattered the right."

"Oh God. That's terrible."

"I woke in a hospital in Miami, where the doctors told me they'd have to take my right leg," Keane continues. "But the last thing I could recall was being on the phone with my mother and I was too worried about her to understand what the doctors were saying."

His story triggers the memory of coming home from work and finding Ben's body on the kitchen floor. It wasn't the tequila and pills that killed him. He'd choked on his own vomit. When I saw him, I fainted, and when I came to, I was convinced I was waking from a nightmare and was so relieved that Ben wasn't really dead, until I saw him a second time.

"Anna, are you okay?"

Tears are pouring down my cheeks and snot trickles from my nose. I wipe my face with my hand, laughing a little. "Of course you'd be more worried about your mom than your leg."

"She heard the whole thing as it happened."

"You don't have to explain," I say, rolling onto my side to look at him. "I know what kind of man you are."

When he turns to look at me, we are so close that I'd only have to lean forward to kiss him. His eyes are dark and inscrutable, and he licks his lower lip. I lean in, and I can hear the rush of blood in my head. I can hear the beat of my heart.

"Anna." He lifts his hand and touches my cheek, the pad of his thumb against my lips. "Wait."

I blink, confused. "You don't—"

"Oh aye, I do," he says. "Jesus, you have no idea. But before you go down this road, you need to be certain what you want. If anyone will do, you need to find someone else."

His hand rests lightly on my face and it's a wonder his hand hasn't caught fire from the embarrassment pumping through my veins. I pull back and stand.

"Your pain is still too close to the surface," Keane says. "I mean, just four days ago on Samana you were mourning for Ben. And even now I can't tell if you're crying for me or him. You can't expect me to play rebound to a ghost. I won't do that."

Feeling like a colossal fool, I retreat up the rocks into the cave. I'm pulling on my skirt when I hear a sharp bark from above. And a second. I look up to see the dog peering down through the hole. It barks again, this time more urgently.

"Do you want to come down here?" I scale the ladder. The dog is not wearing a collar, but it is a she. Her brown eyes are bright, and she allows me to carry her down into the cave. I sit cross-legged on the floor and she climbs into my lap, relaxing as if I'm her personal pillow.

"Anna—" Keane comes into the cave but stops abruptly when he sees the dog. "She's lovely," he says, squatting down to scratch behind her light brown ears. "She looks like a terrier, but with those stubby legs, she may be mixed with Corgi. I reckon she's a pot hound."

"A what?"

"There are a lot of strays in the islands," he says. "And many of them get their meals from the locals who feed them what's left of their cooking pots."

"Pot hound. Cute."

"It is, but there's a bit of a population-control issue."

"This place is pretty remote for a dog to be wandering," I say. "Do you think we should take her back to town with us? Maybe there's a rescue organization or shelter."

"At very least, she'll have better opportunities to eat."

I pull on my tank top, then carry the dog out and to the Jeep. Keane follows with what's left of our picnic. I shouldn't have tried to kiss him. I was out of line. But my embarrassment is way too close to the surface to do anything but pretend it never happened.

* * *

The pot hound rescue staff clucks and fusses over the little dog, petting her head and playing name-that-breed, but they are less than thrilled at the prospect of taking her in.

"We have so many," says a frazzled-looking woman with a mass of springy black curls. She introduces herself as Dr. Suzette Brown. "Are you sure you don't want to keep her? We could put her into the system, administer vaccinations and spay her, and adopt her straight back to you. We'll even waive the adoption fee."

"We're on a boat," I say.

She waves her hand dismissively. "Lots of people keep dogs on boats."

"We'll be leaving for the Antilles in a day or two," Keane says. "It can be a wretched crossing."

"The dog will need to stay quiet after her surgery," Suzette says. "Being cabin-bound will be a good way for her to heal."

"But we're not—" I point back and forth from Keane to myself, struggling with how to tell the rescue vet that we're most definitely not a couple, only to find that Keane has wandered off, inspecting leashes and squeaking fetch toys.

"What I'm not hearing," Suzette says, "is that you don't want her."

The dog's warm little body is snuggled against my chest, right over my heart. I can see my life unfolding into one in which I come home to this dog. Until this moment, I haven't been able to see my life unfold at all. She gives me a tiny dry lick near the corner of my mouth, one that says *I am already yours.* I press my face against the short hairs on the top of her head. "I want her."

"You won't regret it." Suzette takes the dog from my arms. "Pot hounds make the best dogs."

I make arrangements to pick up the dog—*my dog*—tomorrow, and Suzette offers to have one of the volunteers download and fill out entry forms for all of the Caribbean islands. "I'll sign off on the medical work myself."

"You would do all that?"

Suzette shrugs. "It takes time and money to care for these dogs, especially if they're not adopted right away. An hour or two of paperwork costs far less than a month or more in foster care."

"We're going to need lifeline netting so she can safely navigate the deck." Keane returns, his arms overloaded with a green nylon collar and matching leash, a bag of dog food, a package of training treats, and a mesh bag of tennis balls. "And it wouldn't hurt for her to have her own life jacket."

"Maybe we should start by giving her a name."

"I might have gotten a bit carried away because I've always wanted a dog," he says. "Or proximity to a dog. I mean, she's your dog."

"We found her together. She can be your dog too."

"Perfect," he says, opening his wallet to pay for the dog supplies. "Because I was thinking that since we found her at the pirate cove, she should have a proper pirate name. I thought maybe we could call her Gráinne"—he pronounces it *grawn-yeh*—"after Gráinne O'Malley the Irish pirate queen of Connacht, who you might know as Grace O'Malley. But that's a bit unwieldy, so perhaps we should call her Queenie."

"You could have just suggested Queenie."

"But how do you feel about the name?" he asks as we walk out of the building to the Jeep. Already I don't like that I have to leave my dog behind.

"I love it."

When we drive back to the marina, Keane and I don't have much to talk about, aside from the dog. Without Queenie as a buffer, I feel ridiculous for throwing myself at him, so when we reach the boat, I retreat into the cabin and hide in the V-berth. The boat shifts as Keane leaves to wash his limb and rinse his prosthesis, leaving me to replay his rejection on an endless loop in my head. Why did I try to kiss him? What would have happened if he'd let me? I stare up through the open hatch until he returns.

"I'm sorry if I embarrassed you," he says quietly, leaning against the narrow doorway into the V-berth. I pretend to be asleep. "Close quarters and spending every waking moment with a person can . . . well, it can be amplifying."

He continues, so I know he knows I'm faking.

"One day the stars will align," Keane says. "And you won't be thinking about Ben, and the next man—whoever he may be—is going to be one lucky bastard."

The floor creaks as he moves away, and I hear the familiar sounds of him removing his prosthesis and getting into bed. He exhales softly. "Good night, Anna."

My thoughts are a jumbled mess. Is he right? Are close quarters to blame? Am I suffering from a kind of anti-kidnapping Stockholm syndrome? Any other explanation would betray Ben's memory and be unfair to Keane. But I can't quell the quiet fear that trying to kiss him wasn't a mistake.

the rain comes (17)

The rain comes as we eat homemade shrimp pizza with Corrine and Gordon aboard *Patience*. It begins with soft splats on the deck and intensifies into a steady tattoo. We relocate from the covered cockpit to their cabin and Gordon's black Lab hides from the thunder in the aft cabin. Queenie—an inflatable pillow around her neck to keep her from licking her stitches—looks at me, bewildered. Yesterday she was roaming free and now she's been drafted onto our weird little team. I wonder if we've done the right thing, taking her away from the only home she's ever known, but I'm comforted by the warmth of her body as she presses against me.

Four days later the rains are still coming down—sometimes a light mist that hangs in the air, and other times so heavy that it feels as though the world is nothing but water. The idea of dry land feels like a memory. We spend the better part of our time trying to stay dry, trying to keep boredom at bay. Keane reads several chapters of *Moby-Dick* before declaring it "utter shite." Corrine teaches us how to play euchre. I train Queenie to pee on a little swatch of carpet in the corner of the cockpit. I send emails to my mom and Carla, assuring them I'm okay. I don't tell them I have a dog because how would I explain when I don't even understand it myself?

Sometimes it feels as if I'm trying to paint over my old life and I feel guilty that Ben isn't one of the new colors. Other times I miss him so much, I want to pack up and catch the first flight home, as if he's waiting for me in Fort Lauderdale. As if running away from his absence isn't the reason I'm here in the first place.

* * *

"We have a decision to make," Keane says as we sit together in the cabin, eating scrambled eggs with leftover lobster from a second dinner with Corrine and Gordon. Today we've officially overstayed our cruising permit for the Turks and Caicos. If we stay longer, waiting for the perfect weather, we'll have to pay an additional three hundred dollars. Despite the rain, I've grown comfortable here, maybe even a little lazy. I dread the crossing. But I'm not sure I can afford to stay.

"This is probably the end of it," Keane says. "Once this system breaks, we should have decent weather for the rest of the trip. Maybe we should wait it out."

"But you need to get to Puerto Rico," I say. "This is slowing you down."

"I am exactly where I want to be, Anna."

My face grows warm, but I don't have the luxury of dwelling on what that means. Not when we have to decide what to do. Not when, really, I already know. He was right about the intimacy that comes with living on a boat. In the past eighteen days,

I have learned that he hops to the toilet at 4:00 A.M., especially if he's had a lot to drink. He eats too fast from years of squeezing in meals aboard racing sailboats. And that he sleeps deepest on his back. We are tuned in to each other's moods. We share meals, chores, and, now, a dog. Sometimes I catch him looking at me with his feelings, bare and unguarded, flickering across his face. I don't understand why he would want a messed-up girl like me. Yet in those moments, when his longing calls to mine, thoughts of Ben always interrupt, reminding me of what I lost.

"If we leave now, the crossing is going to be brutal," Keane continues. "Under the best of circumstances, this is the kind of trip that can wear down your soul. In weather like this, you'll feel as though you've sold it to the devil."

"Do you have enough money to stay?" I say. "Because if I'm going to make it to Trinidad and get back home, I need to be more careful."

"I could pay it," he says. "But it would be dear to me, as well."

"I'm scared of the weather."

"Then let's wait," Keane says. "We'll divide the cost and stay until we get a window."

Queenie jumps up on the cockpit bench and turns her soulful eyes on him. He makes her give him a high five—a work in progress—before giving her a bit of lobster. He looks at me. "What do you think?"

"Can I ask you something?"

"Anything."

"Do you think I can handle the crossing?"

He doesn't blink. Doesn't even consider. "Yes."

"So let's go," I say. "We're ready. Let's go now."

Like the good surrogate mother she's become, Corrine tries to talk us out of leaving. Gordon listens to the weather forecast and quietly suggests we wait, but says that if we're determined to go, we should sail as far as Big Sand Cay and anchor for the night.

"Take it in pieces," he says. "It'll be a bumpy sleep, but it will give you a chance to rest."

Corrine gives us double-bagged loaves of mango bread. Gordon gifts us with a pair of ten-gallon jerricans filled with fuel and warns us to turn back if conditions become unmanageable. The dark green band of precipitation on the TV weather forecast doesn't look manageable to me, but Keane doesn't seem worried. He lashes the fuel cans to the deck and deflates the dinghy. With a knot of doubt settled heavy in my stomach, we motor away from Providenciales.

Waves rise and fall behind us, obscuring and revealing the island as it recedes. We are quiet and my stomach churns mutinously. I have never suffered from anything more than minor nausea since I first started sailing with Ben, but now I'm overtaken by seasickness and salty saliva fills my mouth. I white-knuckle the lifeline, hurling the contents of my stomach into the sea. I heave until I'm empty, and heave some more, my throat burning and my nostrils stinging. The thought of spending three more days in these conditions makes me cry.

"Are you okay?" Keane asks when I sit back down in the cockpit.

"No." My mouth tastes sour with vomit.

"Do you want to go back?"

There is nothing on earth I would like more than to turn this boat around and return to Providenciales, but sailing was what

I signed on for when I took Ben's boat. I struck a bargain with Keane to help me, not do all the work for me. Still, it's tempting to go back. Skip the crossing entirely. "No."

We take turns on the tiller, giving each other breaks for food and the bathroom, and to check on Queenie. Keane rigged up a little nest for her in the alcove beneath the V-berth. We don't talk much and nearly everything I eat comes back up, leaving me hungry and miserable for the eleven hours it takes to reach Big Sand Cay.

The deserted island of sand provides scant protection from the wind and waves. Queenie bravely pees in the cockpit, but I feel guilty for putting her through this and wish we'd never taken her from Provo. I try to play ball with her in the cabin, but the pain medication for her stitches wears her out, so I bring her into bed with me for the night, hoping I don't puke all over her.

Keane gives me the first watch the next morning, but the sky is so thick with gray that there is little difference from night. Lightning crackles along the horizon as he carries Queenie down into the cabin, leaving me alone on deck. The waves are the largest I've ever encountered—six-foot swells we endlessly dip and climb, dip and climb. I don my harness, clip myself to the jack lines, and stare at the horizon as my stomach churns, trying to keep from throwing up. A losing battle.

Keane brings me a pair of seasickness tablets, which come up before they've even had a chance to go down. He brings me two more, along with a gallon of Gatorade that I sip while my fingertips shred inside his sailing gloves. The muscles in my arms grow sore as I fight to keep the boat on course. There is no pleasure for me in this kind of sailing and no lies that will trick my brain into believing otherwise. This is miserable and painful, and when

Keane comes on deck for his turn at the helm, I am overjoyed my watch has ended. He, on the other hand, is cheerful. Ready to do battle with the ocean, to do this sport he loves.

With Queenie's muzzle resting on my thigh, I sit in the warm, dry cabin and dab antibiotic gel on my blisters and wrap my fingers in gauze. After a week of real meals, a cup of noodles feels like shabby fare. My stomach is concave with hunger. After I've eaten, I play tug-of-war with Queenie using one of Keane's old T-shirts tied into knots. Then I take her up into the V-berth, where we fall asleep.

* * *

"Why didn't you wake me?" I ask Keane as I hand him the Captain America mug filled with coffee. It's become his mug of choice and seeing him use it doesn't bother me anymore. He stood a double watch—eight hours straight—while I slept. Behind Keane, a wave looms, almost as tall as him, and I have to look away to keep my stomach from lurching. Over and over we are scooped up by the waves and lifted to the crest, before we slide back down into the trough. It's a slow, relentless roller-coaster ride.

"I've been enjoying myself," he says, shouting over the wind.

"You have a very weird idea of fun," I shout back.

"Maybe, but it's all I've ever known." He laughs to himself. "You'd be surprised how many girlfriends I've abandoned to appease the wind gods."

"How many?"

"Every last one of them," he says. "Things are grand for a while, but then I need to go sailing. It's no fault of theirs. It's just . . . it's in my blood."

"Your blood is ridiculous."

"You'll have to tell me something I don't know." He stands, my cue to take over the tiller. I'm nervous about doing a night watch but remind myself it's only four hours. I can handle it. "I'm going to sleep and give the leg a bit of airing out, but if you need me, give a shout."

The moon is obscured by clouds, the stars covered, and the night is oppressively dark. There is no moonlight bouncing off the waves, only the red and green running lights on the bow, crashing through the surf. Water washes down the sides of the deck into the cockpit and swirls down the scuppers. Just when the cockpit is drained, the boat plows into the next wave. My face is coated in sea spray, and like this morning, I have to fight the tiller to stay on course. I consider starting the engine to motor-sail for a while, but we don't have enough gas to get all the way to San Juan. We have to save the fuel as a last resort. Despite everything, this is not.

Three-quarters through my watch, I attempt to eat a crumbled slab of mango bread. Nausea rises up almost immediately and I ease myself toward the cooler for the bottle of Gatorade. A wave broadsides the boat and throws me hard against the lifeline. I grab hold, but the next wave hits harder and hurtles me over the line, into the sea.

Beneath the surface I am panicked and disoriented.

Thrashing.

Unable to tell if I'm upside down or right side up.

The water is pitch black and the salt stings my eyes as I struggle to find the surface with no moon to guide me. My harness is still attached and when the boat lifts on the next wave, I slam sideways against the hull. Pain flashes from my shoulder to my fingertips, and my left arm refuses to cooperate as I try to pull myself along the harness line to the surface. The harness jerks and once more I'm lifted from the water. I grab a breath of air and the next second I'm smashed headfirst against the boat.

Stars shimmer behind my eyes.

I see my life unfold in bright flashes.

I see Ben.

Darkness pulls at the edges of my consciousness and I know that I am going to drown. My lungs burn from holding my breath. I can't hold on, but I know that I don't want to die to be with Ben. I would rather live without him.

foundering (18)

My eyes open to the soft golden glow of the cabin lights and Keane's face hovering above mine, his dark brows knit together by worry and fear. The left side of my face pulses as if my heart has shifted into my cheek, and I feel a dizzying rush of blood to my head when I try to sit up. But unless my version of heaven includes Keane Sullivan, I am not dead.

"Who is steering the boat?" My throat feels as if I've been eating sandpaper and he hands me a tumbler of water. The boat pitches on the waves and I hear the sails flapping in the wind. The answer is no one. We are foundering.

"You fell overboard." Keane ignores my question. "Do you remember?"

"No," I say at first, but memory clicks into place and I recall being tumbled like clothes in a dryer and salt water choking my lungs. "I mean, yes. Some of it. What happened?"

"I woke when the boat veered off course," he says. "When I heard thumps against the hull, I scrambled topside and hauled you out of the water." He is not wearing his prosthesis. Pulling me from the water and getting me down into the cabin was nothing short of heroic. "I don't think you've broken your cheekbone, but it's swollen and bruised. You've dislocated your shoulder and likely have a concussion."

From the corner of my eye I see the bump protruding beneath my misshapen shoulder, and the pain is a sustained throb that sharpens when I try to move my arm. I don't look squarely at the damage because my mouth is already pre-vomit salty and I'm afraid I will faint. I close my eyes and take a few deep breaths through my nose until the nausea subsides.

"This may hurt, so I apologize in advance." Keane takes a roll of bandages from the first aid kit. "I would reset your shoulder myself, but I fear doing more damage than good. I'll immobilize it until we can get to a doctor."

He wraps the bandage snug around my shoulder before fashioning a sling from a blue bandanna to hold my arm against my chest. His fingers are gentle as he knots the sling behind my neck. My vision blurs with tears. "You saved me again."

"It's not as if I had another option, Anna."

A small wet laugh slips out at the Keane-ness of his answer. "Thank you."

"Anytime." He tucks a strand of damp hair behind my ear and kisses my forehead. "Every time."

"I want to go home."

I am both healed and broken by the storm. Reminded how

good it is to be alive, but tired of chasing after something I'm never going to catch. I don't know what my life will look like without Ben, but it doesn't have to be the pursuit of his dreams.

"Okay." The word falls heavy from Keane's mouth and I hear his disappointment. "But we're far beyond making landfall in the Dominican Republic and we can't turn back. We have to press on to San Juan."

"I guess I don't have a choice."

We are still two and a half days from Puerto Rico, but the silver lining is that they have good hospitals and cheap nonstop flights to Fort Lauderdale.

"We have a bit of a problem," Keane says. "My knees are aching, and if I don't keep my limb clean, I run the risk of skin breakdown. If that happens, we're fucked. So I'll stand watch in ten-hour shifts if you'll do two, but I can't do this alone."

I wish we could pick up the VHF radio and make a distress call. Abandon this ship. But a dislocated shoulder is not life threatening. I will have to manage. "I know."

"Okay," Keane says. "Get some sleep."

I'm awake, with Queenie snuggled up against me on the bed, as he dons his prosthesis and pulls on his weather gear. I'm awake when he climbs out into the cockpit and puts the boat back on course. After that, I'm asleep.

We sail this way for two watch rotations. Before he goes to sleep each time, Keane prepares meals for me and mixes a gallon of Gatorade that he ties to the deck beside the tiller. I want to return the favor and prepare fresh water for him to wash his residual limb, but my shoulder is so swollen and stiff that I can't move my arm. I almost wish he'd risked the damage and reset the dislocation himself. The rest of my body adapts to the waves, but I stick to a regimen of seasickness pills and painkillers, and after twenty-four hours, my head stops thumping, and I feel good enough to suggest I take longer watches so Keane can get more sleep.

"Are you sure?"

The pain in my shoulder is at the bottom end of terrible and I've finally been able to keep down food. The long stretches of sleep have helped. "I'll be okay."

The front passes during the next thirty-six hours. The sea subsides and three-foot waves feel effortless by comparison. We shed our weather gear as the rain stops for good, and by the time the green mountains of Puerto Rico come into view, the sky has cleared and the sun dries us out. We are dead on our feet. And the dog hasn't shit in three days, but we made it.

We made it.

* * *

I turn on my cell phone for the first time since we left Bimini as we motor past old town San Juan and turn into the cruise ship–lined San Antonio Channel. The phone pings almost nonstop with texts and voicemails, but I ignore the messages to call for a dock at one of the local marinas and arrange for customs check-in.

"I know the customs office is busy," I tell the dockmaster. "But I have a dislocated shoulder and need to get to a hospital, so if there is any way to expedite the process, can we please make that happen?"

The customs officer arrives as Keane and I are securing the spring lines to the dock. We are wedged between a couple of huge fishing boats and the guys aboard them remind me of ChrisDougMike. Three and a half weeks seems like such a very long time ago, especially after the four days we've just had.

The officer inspects our passports and boat documentation and verifies that Keane's green card is valid. He issues a cruising sticker and collects the user fee. He even offers to drop me off at a nearby clinic.

"Do you want me to come?" Keane asks.

"Queenie needs a run."

"Shall I book you a flight back to Fort Lauderdale?"

"Not yet."

He smiles. "Does this mean—"

"I might like to spend Christmas in the Caribbean."

"I can make that happen."

I throw a grin at him over my good shoulder as I follow the customs officer down the dock. "I'm sure you can."

The clinic is about five minutes from the marina, but I fall asleep with my head against the cool window of the air-conditioned car. The officer wakes me up and helps me into the building. Once inside, I fill out the paperwork and call my mom from the waiting room.

"Oh, thank God," she says before I even have a chance to say hello. "Where are you?"

"I just arrived in San Juan. Listen, Mom, I'm at a clinic—"

"What's the matter? Are you hurt?"

"Only a little," I say. "I dislocated my shoulder on the cross-ing, but I'm okay."

"Dislocated?" Her voice goes up an octave, alarmed. "What happened?"

"I—we—hit a wave and I got swept overboard and slammed into the boat a couple of times."

"You could have drowned."

"I could have, but I didn't."

"Anna, I still don't know how I feel about all of this."

"I know, Mom, but I'm fine. Better than fine." And, despite everything, I'm not lying to her. I spent the first part of this trip thinking about what Ben would want. Now I know I have to start thinking about what I want—both here at sea and when I return to my regularly scheduled life. The only thing I know for sure is that making it this far is an accomplishment—*my* accomplishment—and I'm not ready to go home yet. "I'm happy."

"Will you be back in time for Christmas?"

"I'm afraid not." A nurse in pink scrubs calls my name. "Mom, I have to go, but I'll call you back after they fix my shoulder, okay? I love you."

The nurse checks my vitals and unwraps the bandage to have a look at the damage. Pain shoots through me as she helps me remove my T-shirt, raising the hair at the back of my neck and bringing me to tears. My shoulder is twice its normal size and the skin is every shade of a bruise-colored rainbow.

"How long has it gone untreated?" I am relieved she speaks English, because my high school Spanish is so rusty that I could do little more than ask her permission to use the bathroom.

"About three days." I explain how I fell overboard. "We were afraid to set it ourselves."

"I will try to get the doctor in to see you as soon as possible."

I shut my eyes as the examination room door closes behind

her, and don't open them again until I hear a man with a Puerto Rican accent greet me. There is a trail of dried drool on my cheek, and the clock above the door indicates I was asleep for about thirty minutes.

The doctor's accent is thick as he examines my cheek, asking about the pain and the accident. While I recount what happened, he slides on a pair of latex gloves and swabs a bit of alcohol on my upper arm. My shoulder hurts so much that I barely notice the pinch of the needle as he injects a localized painkiller. After the medicine takes hold, the nurse moves over to one side of the exam table and gently restrains me while the doctor takes my arm and pivots outward. I cry out as the muscles in my shoulder twist, but I feel the ball drop back into the socket and the pain lessens, immediately and dramatically.

"You will continue to experience some pain until the swelling goes down, but probably not as severe," he says, scribbling on a prescription pad. The nurse cradles my arm in a proper sling. "I recommend X-rays and a program of physical therapy, but at the very least do not overwork your shoulder. Let it rest for as long as possible."

The doctor hands me a prescription for Vicodin and sends me on my way. As a taxi shuttles me back to the marina, I'm relieved my mother's health insurance will cover most of the expenses, relieved to be mostly back to normal.

Keane is asleep in the V-berth, stripped down to shorts and a T-shirt, his prosthesis removed and Queenie's chin on his foot. I climb into bed and he lifts his arm for me to spoon up in front of him. We've never slept together like this, but it feels good to have his warm chest pressed against my back.

"You smell terrible, Anna." His words come out in the middle of a yawn. "Truly awful."

"So do you."

Keane laughs and wraps his arm tighter around me. "We're a big stinky mess," he says. "All three of us."

"When we wake up, we can all have baths, but for now I just need to sleep for about six days."

"Yeah," he says, yawning again. "Me too."

all I have is now (19)

After the sleeping, the showering, the laundry, the grocery shopping, and the clearing away of the detritus from four days at sea, we celebrate our arrival in San Juan with cold beer and a bowl of homemade guacamole. We have Bob Marley singing about three little birds. Queenie's lifeline netting is installed so she can roam the deck at will. And my shoulder feels a million times better.

Keane and I sit across from each other in the cockpit, his feet propped beside me and mine beside him. Queenie sits next to him, pinning him with a stare meant to intimidate him into giving her a tortilla chip. He strokes her freshly washed head but ignores her relentless gaze.

"What made you decide to stay?" he says.

"I don't know." I scoop a huge portion of guacamole onto a chip. "I guess I figured if I made it this far, there's no sense in turning back."

"The hardest part is behind you."

He means the sailing, but the same could be applied to Ben. I've lived so many hard days since his suicide. Waking up to emptiness. Holding on to pain. Having a future without him still feels scary—and a little unfair to his memory—but it's time to move forward. "So, what are you going to do now?"

"Well, about that..." Keane scratches the back of his head. "When I told you I had to get to Puerto Rico, it was...not entirely true."

"Not entirely?"

"It's a convenient enough place to land," he says. "But there's no real reason I need to be here."

"No guy who knows a guy?"

Keane shakes his head.

"So you helped me just...because?"

"You were a mess, Anna."

I laugh. "Well, I'm still a mess, so maybe you should stay."

Keane's eyes meet mine. "Only if you're asking."

I could laugh it off as a joke and release him from his service, but these past weeks have knocked the rust off my life. Keane has helped me become a sailor. He's also pulled me out of the emotional black hole I've been living in since Ben died. If I ask Keane to stay now, it's not because I need him. "I'm asking."

The corner of his mouth tilts up and he nods. "Then I'm staying."

"What do people do for fun around here?"

"We could walk around Old San Juan and look at the Christmas lights, if you're up for it," he suggests. "Maybe get some dinner. I've only been here once, briefly, on a delivery job."

"That's different."

"What?"

"You not being the expert."

"San Juan is a bit too developed for my tastes," he says. "Give me a surf shack on a rough-and-tumble coastline and I'm a happy man. But I wouldn't mind seeing the Christmas lights. Down here in the tropics, it's easy to forget about the holidays."

I reach into the cooler for a couple of fresh bottles of beer and notice a man walking toward us on the dock carrying a red duffel with an airline baggage tag on the handle. There's a familiarity to his stride, but before I can connect the dots, he waves and calls out, "They told me I might find my brother down here, but all I see is a bog warrior from County Kerry."

Keane's laugh is loud and joyful. "It would take one to know one, wouldn't it?"

He practically leaps off the boat into a grinning, backslapping hug. This man looks like an older version of Keane, a few inches shorter and slightly thicker around the middle. Definitely a Sullivan.

"Anna," Keane says as I step onto the dock, Queenie at my heels. "This bastard would be my brother Eamon. Eamon, meet Anna Beck."

Eamon Sullivan pulls me into a hug as if we're old friends. "Now I understand why my little brother didn't want to come home for Christmas this year. He wrote that you were a fine bit of stuff, but that doesn't do you justice."

Color creeps up the back of Keane's neck. "I did *not* call her a fine bit of stuff."

"No, you didn't," Eamon says. "You said she was beautiful."

"Jesus, you've got a big mouth."

Eamon laughs like an older brother whose teasing hit the mark—and he sounds so much like Keane that it's kind of surreal. Eamon winks at me. "He wasn't wrong."

"I apologize for my brother," Keane says. "He doesn't often stray from the bog, so he doesn't know how to behave in polite society."

They dissolve into laughter again and hug each other once more.

"Permission to come aboard?" Eamon says.

"Granted." I gesture toward the cockpit and scoop up Queenie. She's better at getting out of the boat than getting back in. "Come sit. Have a beer."

"If you continue saying such things, Anna, I'll have to propose."

Keane opens a round of beers and we sit in the cockpit, listening to Eamon talk about the family back home in Ireland. His accent is bolder, and he talks faster than Keane, so I can't always keep up, but I work out that everyone is meeting at the pub for Christmas dinner and they all miss Keane, even Claire.

"Mom would have packed a goose and black puddings if she could," Eamon says, opening his duffel. "But she did send along fruit scones for your birthday and I've brought something even better."

He pulls out a bottle of Irish whiskey and Keane inhales with reverence. "I take back every evil thought I've ever had about you, Eamon. You're the best brother in the world."

"And although it's not Christmas yet, I've also brought something for Anna."

Eamon reaches back into his duffel like a sailboat Santa and pulls out a device that resembles an oversized TV remote.

"Is that . . . an autopilot?"

"It is," he says.

"You bought an autopilot for a stranger?"

"Not exactly. I know a guy."

"Keane said the same thing when he showed up in Nassau with an outboard motor. Am I sailing the Caribbean with stolen goods?"

"Oh no," Eamon says. "Nothing so nefarious as all that. There was a man at the sailing club who was selling it and I had something he wanted, so we made a trade."

"Does it work?"

Keane snorts a laugh and we share a smile.

"Aye, it does." Eamon hands me the device. "But my brother thought since you still have many a mile between here and Trinidad, it might come in useful."

I sit, not knowing what to say, until finally: "Are all of you Sullivans this nice? I thought Keane was some sort of weird anomaly, but this—God. I can't accept this."

"Of course you can."

"Take it," Keane says. "Otherwise you'll never hear the end of it. Truly. He'll be a terrier on the leg of your trousers about it." He glances at the dog. "No offense, Queenie."

"Okay, then," I say. "Thank you."

"You're welcome. Now, I've spent too many hours sitting on planes," Eamon says. "I'm ready for some fun."

I wear my sequined skirt with a white T-shirt and a pair of ankle boots because tonight feels festive. A night for making new memories. Some of the more permanent boats in the marina have colored lights strung through the rigging and Christmas trees lit on deck.

Keane holds Queenie's leash as we walk down the narrow cobbled Calle San Francisco, where the buildings look like colorful layer cakes—red beside yellow beside lime green beside purple—and the balconies are bedecked with red ribbons and swags of pine garland. Music spills from the doorway of every shop. The plazas—de Armas at the west end of the street and de Colón at the east—are decorated with huge Christmas trees. The gazebo in the Plaza de Armas serves as a manger for almost life-size Nativity figures, and the statue of Christopher Columbus in the Plaza de Colón is surrounded by lights in the shape of poinsettias and bells and stars. Old San Juan is covered in lights.

"I've never seen so much Christmas."

Eamon laughs. "It's a bit like old Saint Nick shite himself."

"It's beautiful," I say, and I'm struck by the idea that I could stay here. Get a job at Starbucks and live in a colorful apartment overlooking a cobbled alley in a town that looks like it was transplanted from Europe. But every place I've visited has offered something new and unexpected. And there are so many islands I have yet to see.

"How does tapas sound?" Keane brings me back to the moment, outside a restaurant with sidewalk seating. "There are other people with dogs here, so I reckon they don't mind."

"Sounds perfect."

Eamon orders a pitcher of red sangria and our first round of small plates—ham croquettes with a guava rum glaze, seafood flatbread, and seared octopus salad—and it takes a second for my brain to catch up with my body. I am more than a thousand miles from home, sampling new foods with two men I wouldn't have met if I'd stayed in Fort Lauderdale. It's wild and exciting. If Ben were here, none of this would be happening. I can't even speculate anymore on what my life would be like with Ben because all I have is now.

"Everything okay?" Keane gives my hand a gentle squeeze beneath the table, and when Queenie notices the movement, her wet nose reminds me that tonight is about new memories.

"Yeah." When I smile, I mean it. "Everything's great."

We share the food, kill the pitcher of sangria, and Eamon orders more. The night grows softer until the world twinkles around me, and the ring of my cell phone startles me. It's been silent for so long. The screen says MOM and I realize I forgot to call her back.

"Hi, Mom. Check this out." I press the FaceTime button and pan my phone along Calle San Francisco so she can see Old San Juan. I introduce her to Keane and Eamon, who lift their glasses in a toast, and lower the phone so she can meet Queenie. Then I turn off FaceTime so she can't worry about my bruised cheek. "I know I forgot to call you back, but—"

"You're not coming home, are you?"

"Not until after I get to Trinidad."

"And you're really happy?"

"More than I've been in a long time," I say. "How are you?"

"I'm watching Maisie tonight," she says. "Your sister is on a date. He seems like a real nice guy."

Rachel and Brian—Maisie's father—have been fighting and reuniting for years. Maybe my sister deserves some new memories too. "I hope he is."

"I'm still going to worry about you."

"I know." The waiter returns with beef-and-chorizo sliders, garlic shrimp taquitos, and another pitcher of sangria. "There are worse things in the world than having a mom who loves me enough to worry. We'll talk soon, okay? *Ich liebe dich.*"

While we eat, Eamon tells me about his job, working for a geospatial information firm that provides data for GPS and satellite navigation systems.

"Does that mean you drive the Google Earth car?" I ask, and Keane nearly chokes on his sangria and says, "I've asked him the same thing."

The brothers tell stories about growing up, trying to out-embarrass each other. I laugh a lot and wish I had more to offer in the way of stories, but all my best stories involve Ben. Until now.

It's after midnight when the taxi drops us off at the marina. I'm loose-limbed and sleepy, and when Eamon suggests we crack open the whiskey, I decline. "I'm going to bed."

As they settle into the cockpit with plastic tumblers of Green Spot, I change into my pajamas and crawl into bed. Their quiet laughter mixes with the soft lap of the water against the hull and the musical chime of the halyard clanking against the mast, composing a lullaby that sings me to sleep.

headfirst into life (20)

The sun is wide-awake when I get up the next morning, but the Sullivan brothers are not. The cabin reeks of whiskey breath. Eamon is passed out in Keane's bed while Keane sleeps scrunched up on the side berth like a little boy. I carry Queenie up the companionway ladder, clip on her leash, and we hustle across the busy highway that runs in front of the marina. On the other side, we stop-sniff-and-pee our way to the pedestrian fishing pier sandwiched between the spans of the Two Brothers Bridge. From the pier, I call Carla.

"It's about time you called," she says, but I hear the smile in her voice.

"Sorry it wasn't sooner. I had zero bars in the middle of the ocean."

"Where are you?"

"San Juan." Now that I have a strong signal and time to sit, I tell her everything. She offers best friend outrage over Bimini

Chris and demands to see Queenie. I put her on FaceTime, and she calls me a badass when she sees the bruises on my cheek.

"I feel like I don't even know you anymore," she says. "When you left, I thought you were running away, but here you are, running headfirst into life."

"Trust me, I'm just as surprised."

She laughs. "And this guy, Keane. Are you . . . ?"

"Two weeks ago I was so angry at Ben that I was screaming my lungs out on a deserted beach, and I'm not sure I'll ever be over him," I say. "Keane is . . . a friend."

"A hot friend who wants to kiss you."

I laugh. "Shut up."

"Keep running, Anna," Carla says. "Kiss the man if you want to kiss him. Or don't. Just remember that what Ben would want doesn't count anymore."

After we hang up, I sit in the sunshine for a while, watching a man fish. His reel zings out as cars whoosh across the bridges around us, but the pier is still a strangely peaceful spot. When I'm ready—or at least as ready as I'll ever be—I dial Barbara Braithwaite. "It's Anna Beck."

"Hello, Anna." Ben's mother has a way of sounding cool and warm at the same time. At first it left me wondering how she felt about me, but dozens of voicemails demanding that I return the boat before she has me arrested make it much less ambiguous. "Where are you?"

I ignore the question. "I'm not giving you the boat. You can waste your money contesting Ben's will and trying to chase me down, but he left it to me. This boat is mine."

This is the first time I've ever raised my voice to Ben's mother *and* the first time I've called this boat my own. But the Alberg is filled with *my* things, arranged to meet *my* needs. It belongs to me.

"Regardless of what you think of me, I loved Ben more than you'll ever know," I say. "Call off the dogs. For once please respect his decision."

"How dare you—"

I end the call with shaking fingers, not giving her the chance to finish. It doesn't feel good to deny Barbara something she wants, but it doesn't feel bad, either. She can't have everything.

As we walk back to the marina, Queenie stops to poke her nose into the fisherman's empty bucket. I notice some of the larger fishing boats are gone for the day, and when I get back to the sailboat—*my boat*—there is a note tucked into the shackle of the lock.

Gone to mass at the cathedral.

"Of course, you have," I say aloud, and while Keane and Eamon are gone, I clean up the cabin. The boat feels even smaller with Eamon's things aboard. With the boat in order, I cook up a big batch of banana pancakes, keeping them warm in the oven, and feeding bits of banana to Queenie while we wait for the Sullivans to return.

"You can be my little pancake hound," I tell her, and she gives me a dog smile like she understands. I'm glad she's here with me instead of wandering a lonely beach in Providenciales.

"Drop all your plans for the day, Anna," Keane announces when he and Eamon step aboard the boat. They're dressed in church clothes and I pretend not to notice how good they look. Especially Keane. "We've got a surprise for you."

"But I was going to scrub the bilge today," I say, and Eamon chuckles as he peeks in the oven at the pancakes. "Whatever you've got planned better be pretty damn exciting."

Keane hands me a trio of tickets to see the Tiburones de Aguadilla play the Cangrejeros de Santurce. Sharks versus Crabbers.

"Baseball?"

"One of the locals told us after mass that the games are like parties," he says.

"And," Eamon adds, "they sell piña coladas at the stadium."

* * *

Our seats are in the four-dollar bleacher section of the stadium, behind left field, where we're trapped in the glare of the afternoon sun. But what the church local said about Puerto Rican baseball is absolutely true. The game hasn't even begun, and fans are tooting vuvuzelas and rattling thundersticks. People are singing and dancing at their seats, as if they're at the World Series or the Super Bowl.

Cangrejeros are the home team—and their little crab logo is cute—so I buy one of their baseball caps to keep the sun out of my face. The commentators announce the starting lineups in both English and Spanish, and I blink back tears while singing the national anthem with the people sitting around me. I've sailed more than a thousand miles, but this one song on this faraway island makes me feel homesick.

"I must confess." Eamon hands me a piña colada that he bought from the roving stadium vendor. "I have no fucking clue what's going on."

"I don't know a lot about baseball either, but I figure if we cheer when everyone else does, we'll be okay."

There is nothing magical about the game. Except that after four straight days of water, this is exactly what I needed. At the bottom of the ninth inning, when the Crabbers have a healthy lead and I have a healthy buzz, I lean into Keane. "How do you always know?"

"Know what?"

"Everything," I say. "What I need. What I don't."

He shrugs. "I . . . I just do."

I wonder what he was really going to say, but before I can ask, a home run ball rockets toward our corner of the ballpark, and the question is forgotten in a flurry of excitement as the crowd around us scrambles to catch it.

In the cab on the way back to the marina, the three of us are still a little high on tropical drinks when Keane raises the question of Christmas. "Would you like to stay here? Or we could sail to Jost Van Dyke in the BVIs."

"What's happening on Jost Van Dyke?"

"There's a bar that hosts a Christmas party for sailors who are away from home."

"Oh God. I'm keeping you from your family."

"That's not the takeaway here, Anna," Keane says as Eamon pays the cabdriver. "My brother is my family, so I'm sorted. The goal is for you to have a happy Christmas, so whatever you want to do, we'll do."

It's too soon for my body to head back out to sea. My arm is still cradled in a sling and I've only just stopped swaying when standing on dry land. But the longer we stay, the harder it will be to leave. San Juan lulls me, makes me feel at home. "We should go."

"Are you sure?"

"Yes."

Eamon walks with Queenie and me to the marina office to settle the bill. At the counter, he opens his wallet and plunks down a credit card. He has paid for nearly everything in San Juan and I don't feel comfortable with that.

"I wish you wouldn't," I say.

"It's nearly Christmas," he says. "And I'd have spent far more on a hotel room."

"You brought me an autopilot."

He waves me off. "It's been a very good year for me, Anna, and you have a long way to go. Please let me do this."

"I don't understand how you and your brother can be so kind."

"It's uncomplicated, really," Eamon says. "Our mother expected us to be good and our father put the fear of the Lord in us if we failed to meet her expectations. That doesn't mean we don't act the maggot sometimes, but kind is one of the easiest things to be."

"Thank you."

He slides his credit card back into his wallet, signs the receipt, and kisses my forehead the same way Keane does, making me think it's another Sullivan family habit. "Let's call ourselves square."

* * *

The sail from Puerto Rico to Jost Van Dyke is long, but nothing like the big crossing. The air is the perfect mix of warm and cool, the sea is calm, and with the autopilot doing most of the work, we have little to do but trim the sails. Keane estimates it will take around twelve hours, but having a crew of three means we don't have to break the time into shifts. We can sleep whenever we like, but mostly we sit on deck, pass around a bottle of wine, and talk.

Around midnight I walk up to the foredeck to sit with my back against the cabin. Queenie follows and climbs into my lap. The sea and sky are deep velvet blue, melting together at the horizon, and I lose count of the shooting stars. The distance is dotted by the red and green running lights of boats heading toward the Virgin Islands.

Keane comes up, leaving Eamon alone in the cockpit. "Mind if I join you?"

I shift, making space for him to lean. "Doing okay?"

"I was about to ask you the same."

"How are your knees?"

"Fit," he says. "I've had a chance to rest, so I'm set to rights. How's the shoulder?"

"The swelling has gone down and regular pain reliever seems to be doing the trick, but it's stiff and I have this irrational fear that if I move too much, it will pop back out of the socket."

"Highly unlikely," Keane says. "But it's not a bad idea to ginger it until it heals."

"True. So, tell me about Christmas on Jost Van Dyke."

"Foxy's Bar serves a special holiday menu. Fancy stuff like tenderloin, swordfish, and even lobster. If you consider lobster fancy."

I laugh, remembering the conversation about the fanciness of lobster. It seems like a lifetime ago.

"They'll have a musician to play Christmas music, both traditional carols and Caribbean songs," he continues. "Most folks cruising the islands during the holidays don't have a place to go, so Foxy provides."

"I miss my family more than I expected," I say. "My mom was hurt when I left, but now that we've had a chance to talk . . . Well, I won't get to see my niece open her presents this year."

"Maybe you could pick out some gifts for your family along the way and have a second Christmas when you get home."

"That's a good idea."

"Every now and again I have one," he says. "The other thing I wanted to tell you is that I have friends on Jost Van Dyke who have opened their home to us, so we won't have to sleep on the boat. Unless, of course, you'd rather."

"If you think I'm going to turn down a real bed, you are *so* wrong."

We sit in companionable silence, and Queenie steals from my lap into his, nuzzling his hand for attention. Once in a while the boat cuts through a wave that sends a fine mist over us, but it dries almost as quickly as it lands.

"The foredeck was once my domain," Keane says finally. "Calling the start, sails up and down, setting the spinnaker. I was fast, Anna. I was so fucking fast, but now . . ." When he trails off, I don't have the right words to snap him out of his melancholy.

"What boat owner wants a has-been with a prosthetic leg when he can have an able up-and-comer?" The bitterness in his voice makes me want to cry, especially when I've seen what he can do. "They're all very kind about it, but the writing's on the wall in huge fucking letters. You're done, Sullivan. But I can't stop wanting it."

"Maybe—"

"After the accident I set a deadline for myself," he continues. "If I wasn't working as a professional sailor again by the time I turned thirty, I'd give up the pursuit. For what? I have no idea, but my birthday is in one week and here we are."

I'm grateful he interrupted me, because offering unhelpful suggestions isn't what he needs any more than I needed them after Ben died. I know how it feels to want something you can no longer have.

"The thing is," Keane says, "if I am completely truthful, the last three weeks have been the happiest I've had in a good long while—your brush with death notwithstanding—but this is not how I imagined my life."

"Me either."

"Perhaps our paths were meant to cross."

"Stranger things have happened."

He laces his fingers through mine and I let him. Keane doesn't ask for anything more and we fall into a silence that lasts until pale light gathers along the horizon. In the night we sailed above Isla Culebra—one of the Spanish Virgins. To the south is St. Thomas in the US Virgins. Ahead, the hills of Jost Van Dyke rise black out of the water.

"I should probably go spell my brother." Keane releases my hand and puts Queenie back in my lap.

"I'll come with."

Eamon is wide-awake and wired, an insulated mug of coffee in his hand and a broad grin across his face. "I haven't sailed like this since we were kids. This is fucking fantastic."

"You ready for a nap?"

"Not yet," he says. "But I wouldn't say no to breakfast."

I offer to cook, but Keane goes below and soon I hear him whistling his breakfast-making tune. I bring out Queenie's carpet so she can do her morning business, then feed her a bowl of kibble. After having scrounged for leftovers, she still devours the food as though it's her last meal. She's tearing the fuzz off one of her tennis balls when Keane hands up plates heaping with eggs, fried salami, toast, potatoes, and beans.

"Nearest I could come to a proper Irish fry without rashers, sausage, and puddings," he says, but Eamon devours his food nearly as fast as Queenie.

The sun rises behind the island, turning the sky gold behind the hills. I wash up the dishes, while Keane takes over the tiller and Eamon naps in the cockpit. We sail until we reach the mouth of Great Harbour, then motor into the anchorage. Keane and Eamon go below to nap while I take the dinghy ashore with our passports and Queenie's health certificate to clear customs. After I've paid the fees, I return to the boat, raise the British Virgin Islands courtesy flag, and crash-land in my bed.

a patchwork house (21)

Jost Van Dyke is a small, sparsely populated island that slopes from beach to hills without stopping, yet the harbor is filled with boats and the beachfront bars are busy with people as we lock the dinghy and carry our bags up the road to wait for our ride.

"Felix and Agda live right up on Man O' War Hill," Keane says, pointing to a house on the ridge. "Wait until you see it up close. You'll never want to leave."

Two minutes later an old blue Toyota Land Cruiser comes to a stop in front of us, its driver a shirtless man about Eamon's age with a shock of white-blond hair and a raccoon mask of untanned skin around his eyes. The door flings open and he bounds out, his feet bare, to hug Keane.

"Welcome! Welcome to Jost Van Dyke." Felix has yet another new accent for me to figure out. It's not Caribbean, but it's also not Irish or American. He opens the back of the Land Cruiser for us to throw in our gear. "Sullivan, Agda said to come straight back to the house instead of stopping for a drink because she is eager to see you."

Once we're all inside, the Land Cruiser bumps up the unfinished road and Felix gives us a rundown on the island since Hurricanes Irma and Maria devastated the British Virgin Islands. "Great Harbour lost a lot of vegetation and the Methodist church was ruined. But most of the bars and shops have been rebuilt, and new palm trees have been planted. We lost some of our roof, but life goes on, you know?"

Felix explains that he and his wife run a dive charter business. Unlike the crew on *Chemineau*, they have a waiting list of clients. "We just returned from Belize, so your timing is very good." He laughs. "Our home is still clean."

The house at the top of Man O' War Hill looks as if it was built in sections, tacked on over time and painted whatever color they happened to favor at the moment, which Felix explains is exactly what happened. "It's a strange house, I know," he says. "When we first moved here from Sweden, we could not afford to build more than a one-room shack."

As goofy as the place looks on the outside, the inside is beyond inviting. The floors are planked with dark, soft wood, and every single room has a balcony overlooking Great Harbour and the surrounding forested hills. "This is amazing."

"See what I mean?" Keane says.

The furniture looks like it was acquired piecemeal, and from different places around the world. The threadbare gold velvet couch is draped with a multicolored Peruvian blanket, similar to the cushions on my boat. Diving magazines are piled on an African drum. And a huge aboriginal artwork takes up most of one wall.

Another wall is covered with photos of Felix and Agda—usually wearing scuba gear—in various oceans.

"Agda!" Felix calls out. "Sullivan has arrived."

The sound of bare feet slapping on the wood floor greets us, then a flash of red dress and white-blond hair as she flings herself into Keane's arms. "It is so wonderful to see you," she squeals as he spins her around. She is bony and wholesome and has the same Scandinavian features as Felix. I'm in awe of the whiteness of their hair, until I catch my own reflection in a mirror. The color has been leached from my braids by the sun while my skin is darker than it's ever been.

"Agda, this is Anna," Keane says. "We are traveling together to Trinidad."

"It's good to meet you, Anna."

"Likewise."

"Come with me." She calls the words over her shoulder, already in motion. "I will show you to your room."

The balcony serves as the hallway for the house, and I follow Agda to the end, where French doors stand open, inviting the sun and air into the bedroom. The bed seems enormous after weeks at sea and the blanket on top is a patchwork of old wool sweaters. A patchwork quilt for a patchwork house. My grubby bag on the floor is like a sliver of thumb across the corner of an otherwise perfect photo.

"This room is best because it has its own water closet." She pulls back a white shower curtain in the corner to reveal a toilet and tiny wall sink. "And it is closest to the shower."

She leads me back outside. Beside my room is an outdoor

shower built of wood with a yellow canvas curtain. "My favorite time is when you are showering and it begins to rain."

"This house is bizarre."

Agda laughs. "It is bizarre, but we love it."

"Me too."

"I will leave you to shower or sleep or whatever you would like to do," she says. "We have Wi-Fi if you need to write emails, and later we will go to Foxy's for Christmas dinner, yeah?"

"Thank you."

Agda smiles in reply and suddenly I'm alone. Keane finds me leaning against the balcony railing, trying to pick out the Alberg in the fleet of cruising boats moored in the harbor.

"Now that I'm finally thinking of it as my boat, it needs a name."

"Don't think too hard about it," he says. "Boats reveal their names to you in good time."

"Did you make that up?"

He nods. "It's a solid theory, though, right?"

"I'm going to go try out that shower."

"I wanted to warn you," he says. "Agda typically walks naked to and from the bath."

"Good to know, thanks."

"You could do the same, if you like. When in Rome and such."

"Shut up."

He laughs as he bumps his shoulder against mine. "Don't use all the hot water."

Not nearly as brave as Agda, I draw the yellow curtain across the shower, but above me the sky is midmorning blue and the air is cool on my skin. Even though I can hear everyone's indistinct chatter at the other end of the balcony, I can't help feeling alone. This is my first Christmas without Ben. I turn off the faucet, but my thoughts keep flowing. I put on his old *How the Grinch Stole Christmas!* T-shirt, faded green and worn soft, and a red polka-dot skirt more festive than I feel.

"Anna, you are so cute! You are the Grinch." Agda pours a glass of pink rum punch and slides it across the table to me as I sit. "Eamon has been trying to explain his job to me and I can't get my brain around it. So, you tell me what you do."

"Well, right now, I just . . . sail." I look past her at the harbor and take a deep breath. "My fiancé died by suicide almost a year ago, and I was having a hard time dealing with it, so I quit my job, took his sailboat, and left."

"About your fiancé, I am very sorry," she says, touching the back of my hand with light fingers. "But it is a very brave thing you are doing."

"I'm not so sure about that." My laugh isn't entirely genuine, but I don't want to cry. "After I nearly got hit by a cargo ship on my very first crossing from Florida to Bimini, I realized I had no idea what I was doing and hired Keane."

"See, now I know you are brave. Sullivan is a wild man."

I take a sip of rum punch. It's very sweet and very strong, making my eyes water. "How did you all meet?"

"We had a mutual friend who owned a dive shop on Martinique, and we happened to be visiting him at the same time," Keane says. "I was maybe twenty-four or twenty-five, between boats—"

"You were there with that French girl," Agda interrupts. "What was her name?"

"Mathilde."

The people around us are evidence enough that Keane has a history, but Mathilde is History with a capital *H*. Her name conjures the image of another effortlessly cool girl—like Sara on *Chemineau*—who looks perfect in a bikini. And at that age, Keane must have been the human equivalent of a bug zapper.

"Yes! Mathilde!" Agda slaps the table. "I have to tell you, Sullivan, we hated her. She was so dull."

"I reckon I wasn't dating her for her personality," he says dryly. "My personal bar was set pretty low in those days."

Eamon laughs. "What's changed?"

We all wait while Keane drains his punch. The ice cubes rattle in the glass and the air is filled with the sounds of birds and frogs. The legs of his chair scrape on the floor as he pushes back to stand. "Everything."

He walks away, his mood darkened, and Eamon shakes his head. "Always dramatic, that one."

I follow Keane.

He's cycled back to where he was last night on the boat, but given that I've just struggled with my own melancholy, I can't fault him for it. He drops into an old cracked leather chair in the corner of the room he's sharing with Eamon.

"Well," Keane says. "Now I can't go back out there because I'm a fucking idiot."

I perch on the corner of the bed closest to his chair. "If it makes you feel any better, I suffered way too much inner turmoil over wearing this T-shirt."

"Ben?"

"Bingo."

"You look really cute wearing it."

"Thanks." My cheeks warm like I'm standing in a patch of sunshine. I don't want to be flattered when he says things like this, but I am. "You know ... it's Christmas Eve. Maybe we should celebrate what we have instead of thinking about what we don't."

He tries to conceal an oncoming smile. "If I had been as smart at twenty-five as you are, I probably wouldn't have dated Mathilde at all. She really was dull."

all is calm, all is bright (22)

If we're not all in high spirits, we hide it well beneath our Christmas accessories. Felix has donned a navy-blue sweater knit with white reindeers and snowflakes. Agda's short hair is pulled back in a headband with bell-tipped antlers that jingle constantly as the Land Cruiser bounces down the road. Eamon has chosen a Santa hat and announces he'll be inviting single women to sit on his lap, earning a smack on the shoulder from Agda. Even Keane has several red and green strings of Mardi Gras beads draped around his neck.

Like most waterfront bars, Foxy's has tables on the sand and Caribbean music in the air—and tonight there isn't a single un-reserved table in the house. As we weave our way through the restaurant to our table, Agda keeps stopping to hug people.

"Everybody knows everybody else," she explains. "Our island is very small."

The table is on the beach, where tiki torches burn, and a live

Christmas tree stands decorated with lights and ornaments. Two couples are already seated, other friends whose sailboats are anchored in Great Harbour. Jefferson and Karoline Araujo are on their way home to Brazil after a circumnavigation, while Amanda Folbigg and Luke Cross have sailed up from Panama after doing a Pacific crossing that began in Australia. Leaving Fort Lauderdale almost a month ago seemed like a big deal, but sitting among these accomplished sailors, I feel young and green. Like I should be sitting at the kids' table.

Felix orders a round of painkillers, a rum-and-pineapple drink claimed to have been invented on the island, and Amanda asks about my sling. I'm embarrassed to admit I fell overboard, but no one laughs. Luke points out a jagged scar on his forehead. "I failed to duck when the boom swung."

"When I first started out," Keane says, "I crossed the deck a bit too quickly on a tack and slid right under the lifeline. Grabbed on to a stanchion to keep the boat from sailing off without me, but I was dragged along, face-first through the water, until they managed to pull me back aboard."

As we eat our Christmas dinners, everyone seems interested in hearing about my trip and they share their stories about the places Keane and I have been. The conversation never lags, but this time I'm part of it.

"So, Anna, where will you go after Jost Van Dyke?" Agda asks.

"I think Saint Martin."

"Definitely go to the French side," she says. "The Dutch side is overrun by tourists from the cruise ships and Maho Beach is a nightmare."

I don't admit that Ben's original plan included Maho Beach,

which is situated at the end of the airport runway. The incoming planes pass low over the beach before touching down, and the engines from outgoing planes generate so much wind that spectators are blown backward into the water.

"Ugh, yes." Karoline nods in agreement. "It's always crowded, and the novelty wears off after one or two planes. We're all sailing to Saint Barths for New Year's Eve. There will be concerts and parties and fireworks at midnight. You should join us."

Eamon shakes his head. "Probably not the best idea considering—"

"Could be fun," Keane says, cutting him off, and I'm surprised he'd want to go to St. Barths, given his history with the island.

"Are you sure?" Eamon asks.

"It's been five years." The muscle in Keane's jaw twitches and I wonder if this is a brother thing—proving to Eamon that he can handle returning to the scene of the crime.

"Okay." Eamon looks at me. "Anna, you're the captain."

I could overrule Keane, but I don't want to embarrass him, especially since he's no longer my crew. I have to trust that my friend knows what he's doing. "I guess we're sailing to Saint Barths."

After dinner, we shuffle around the table, some going off to dance, while others stay behind and talk. Karoline tells me about her work as an interior design stylist, designing rooms for decorating magazines and personal clients. Her enthusiasm makes me long for . . . something that makes me feel that sort of passion. Something more than being a waitress for the rest of my life.

Keane returns to the table after dancing with Agda, Amanda, and Felix, and downs the remainder of my painkiller in a single swallow.

"Christmas karaoke in five minutes," Eamon says to his brother. "I've signed us up."

Keane shakes his head. "No."

"It's tradition," Eamon says. "Besides, if Anna has thrown her lot in with the likes of you all the way to Trinidad, she ought to know what sort of man you are."

Keane laughs at something only they understand. "Okay. *If we swap parts.*"

"Why ruin a good thing after all these years?"

"I know, but—" He fakes a heavy sigh. Eamon chuckles while the rest of us wonder what the hell is happening. "Fine. I'll do it."

"Do what?" I ask.

"Can't tell you," Keane says. "It'll spoil the magic."

Christmas karaoke kicks off with Foxy himself singing a reggae version of "We Wish You a Merry Christmas" and welcoming everyone to his restaurant. Foxy is followed by a pair of white women performing back-to-back renditions of "White Christmas" and "Winter Wonderland." Both tease out the long notes and throw diva-like hand gestures. On any other day, we might be laughing at their overblown efforts, but tonight we clap like we are at the Grammys.

"It's time." Eamon pushes away from the table and Keane follows. Agda and I squeeze through the crowd to get a front-row view. Eamon picks up a pair of microphones, one of which he hands to his brother.

"Happy Christmas," Eamon says. "We are the Sullivans of County Kerry, Ireland." His introduction is met with applause

and a few whistles—presumably from the Irish in the crowd—
before he continues.

"When I was a lad, I decided it would be a laugh to teach
my baby brother some colorful new words." He gestures at Keane,
earning a few laughs at how much taller he is than Eamon. "So,
while everyone was gathered at our family's pub for Christmas, we
performed a duet. And following a stern lecture about setting a
better example for my brother—"

"A lesson which never stuck, I might add," Keane interjects.

"—we were asked to repeat the song that first year and subse-
quent years since," Eamon says. "It's a time-honored, traditional,
heartwarming Christmas love song passed down through the
ages. If you recognize it, sing along."

The music starts, a few piano notes barely audible over the
noise of the bar, and Eamon begins to sing, his words slurry as
though he's drunk. "*It was Christmas Eve, babe, in the drunk tank—*"

Those in the crowd who recognize the opening line of "Fairy-
tale of New York" by the Pogues start laughing, not only because
it's neither traditional nor heartwarming but also because they
realize Keane will be singing the woman's part.

When it comes, I'm expecting to hear him sing with falsetto,
but Keane doesn't do it. He sings low and slightly off-key, which
makes the song even funnier. By the time the brothers have finished, the whole bar is singing and clapping along.

"Was that story true?" I ask Keane as we go back to the table.
"Eamon really did that to you?"

"Oh aye," Keane says. "I was singing happily along, blissfully
ignorant, until Mom's eyes went as round as dinner plates and

my old hard-of-hearing gran said, 'Did Christopher just call his brother a scumbag? I thought this was a Christmas tune.'"

As I'm laughing, I think about my sister and how long it's been since we've had that much affection for each other. When we were little, we used to put on "shows" for our parents. We'd spend hours coloring backdrops and rehearsing lines that changed every time. Rachel was always the director and I was happy to follow her lead. I don't remember when things changed, but as the conversation around me melts into background noise, I'm nostalgic for the sisters we used to be.

"I'll be right back."

Along the water, hammocks have been strung between palm trees. I find an empty one and ease myself into it. Once it stops swaying, I call home.

"Merry Christmas, Anna," Mom says, and she whispers, "It's Anna." I can imagine my sister rolling her eyes. "Rachel and I are wrapping Maisie's presents and drinking glühwein."

Mulled spiced wine is one of the few family traditions Mom brought with her from Germany. Even when we were little girls, she would let us drink small mugs of glühwein. "That sounds like fun."

"Where are you?"

"On an island called Jost Van Dyke," I tell her. "It's part of the British Virgin Islands."

"Hold on. Let me get my map," she says. "Talk to Rachel."

"Hey." My sister sounds less than thrilled to speak to me.

"You know what I was thinking about?"

"What?"

"When we used to put on shows for Mom and Dad," I say.

"Remember how you would make up songs on the spot and I would try to sing along even though I had no idea what words you were going to sing next? I was always a beat behind."

Rachel laughs through her nose. "I can't believe you remember that."

"I miss you guys." I hold my breath, waiting for a smartass remark.

"It's weird that you're not here."

"What did you get Maisie for Christmas?"

"Glittery shoes and a toy cell phone," she says. "I swear to God, she's two going on twenty."

"Give her a kiss for me and tell her we'll have more Christmas when I get home."

"I will," Rachel says. "Is this helping? What you're doing, I mean? You sound . . . different."

"Yeah, it is."

"I'm glad." The line goes quiet, but the silence isn't awkward or filled with things left unsaid. Maybe this is a temporary truce, but tonight I will settle for all is calm, all is bright. "Mom's back," Rachel says. "Merry Christmas, Anna."

"You've sailed so far," my mom says with a note of wonder.

"A thousand miles, more or less."

"Aren't you afraid?"

"All the time," I admit. "But Keane is with me and he is . . ." I struggle for the words that will encompass everything he's become. Guide. Travel companion. Safety net. Rock. Comfort. Friend. "I wouldn't have gotten this far without him. He's taught me a lot."

"I'm glad you're not alone anymore."

The table is not so far away that I can't hear Agda's big laugh, or the way Karoline claps and shouts "Yes!" whenever she agrees with what someone is saying. I've failed pretty spectacularly at running away. "Me too."

We wish each other *Fröhliche Weihnachten. Ich liebe dich. Gute Nacht.* I end the call as Keane is crossing the sand to my hammock.

"Doing okay there, Anna?"

"Yep."

He gestures toward the opposite end of the hammock. "Room for a plus-one?"

"I only share with people who have saved my life."

"Then I reckon it's my lucky night." The hammock tilts precariously as he climbs in so that we're facing each other. "We should have one of these for the boat. String it up on the foredeck."

"Okay."

"That was too easy."

"My small heart grew three sizes today." I point to my Grinch T-shirt. "Or maybe it's just a good idea."

Keane rests his arm on my shin, his hand on my knee. We've come so far in such a short amount of time. Almost a month ago I suffered anxiety over sleeping in the same cabin. Now we routinely invade each other's space.

"You seem happy," he says.

"I guess I am."

meager offerings (23)

Morning comes early and bright, and I wake to find Queenie sleeping on the pillow beside my head. Nova, a small tan island dog who claims Felix and Agda whenever they're home, is curled on the floor beside the bed. The house is quiet, but the breeze rustles the leaves of the trees and the birdsongs are constant. I get out of bed, and peek into Keane and Eamon's room. It's early for them to be awake and gone, but it's Christmas Day. There's no Catholic church on the island, but I suspect they've gone to services in the makeshift annex beside the ruined Methodist church at the bottom of the hill.

The Christmas tree is a tiny pine in the middle of the coffee table and there are presents strewn around it. Among them are some with my name and I'm embarrassed that I didn't even think about gifts. Not even for Keane.

Agda is awake, her hair sticking out every which way, when I reemerge from my room, dressed to go down the hill and with Queenie on her leash.

"I'm going to check on the boat."

"The Sullivans have the car."

"It's okay," I say. "We'll hike it."

Going downhill doesn't take long with the help of gravity. At the landing, Queenie hops eagerly into the dinghy, and as we motor out to the Alberg, I realize she's becoming a boat dog.

The anchor is secure, so I brew a small pot of coffee for myself and dig through my belongings, searching for potential Christmas presents. There is a bottle of German wine I was saving for Trinidad that I decide to give to Felix. Agda is a bigger challenge because I don't feel right giving my clothes—even lightly worn—to someone who has welcomed me into her home. On the top shelf of the hanging locker is Ben's Polaroid. He loved that camera, but I haven't used it since he died. I take the camera from the shelf, brush off the dust, and snap a picture of Queenie.

Keane is the hardest of all because I have nothing to offer him. Except, sitting in the sink is the Captain America mug. My heart aches a little as I carefully wash and dry it, and I begin to understand why Ben's mother swept in after his death and took everything she could get her hands on. But the mug is not Ben and giving it to Keane will not diminish his memory.

I gather everything into a paper shopping bag and sit on deck until my coffee is gone. When Queenie and I return to shore, Foxy's gift shop has opened for the day and I buy a T-shirt for Eamon.

I perch on the tile steps of the empty, gutted church with my dog and my gifts, close my eyes, and listen to the pastor's voice drift out from the nearby annex, sermonizing about a manger in Bethlehem. Perhaps my meager offerings will be enough.

The pastor comes out first, the congregation singing "O Come, All Ye Faithful" behind him, and I move Queenie away from the path of the procession as they walk by.

"It's okay," he says. "Everyone is welcome. Merry Christmas."

Keane and Eamon are among the first people who stream out from the annex and they're surprised to see me.

"I wanted to make sure the boat was okay," I say. "But I could use a lift up the hill."

Back at the patchwork house, I wrap presents using borrowed paper and add them to the pile around the little tree. Felix is awake and we all gather in the living room for the exchange. We crisscross each other as we hand things out, so my first gift is a pink Foxy's T-shirt from Eamon. He laughs when he opens the men's version of the shirt in black. "It's the stuff of O. Henry stories, isn't it?"

From Agda I receive the striped hammock from her balcony. "Sullivan said you'd like one, and we're going back to Belize after the holidays, so we can buy another."

She unwraps the camera and I don't tell her it belonged to Ben. I smile as she clicks a picture of Keane and me sitting on the golden couch, his arm stretched out along the back behind my shoulders. Agda gifts him a vintage Guinness T-shirt with a toucan on the front that she found in a charity shop in Belize, and Felix is inundated with bottles of Irish whiskey, German wine, and Puerto Rican rum.

Soon all that's left is Captain America. Keane unwraps the mug and a wrinkle of confusion forms between his eyebrows.

"It was Ben's favorite," I say. "But you use it so much that I don't really see it as his anymore. So I figured . . . Well, maybe someday when you're off on some remote island, you'll fill it with coffee and think of me."

He turns the mug over in his hands. "Are you sure?"

"I want you to have it."

"This is grand, Anna, thank you." Keane leans over and kisses my temple. "I, uh—I wish I had something for you, but I—"

"Saving my life is enough."

The rest of Christmas Day unfolds lazily: a breakfast of Swedish pancakes topped with lingonberry sauce, naps, and lots of sprawling in various places around the house. When I go to the bathroom, there is a small stain in my underwear, a reminder that I've been away from home for a month. And another thing I never thought about having to manage while living on a sailboat.

On Boxing Day, Felix drives us around the island, jostling along roads that—in some places—are little more than dirt tracks. We stop at the bubbly pool, a natural tidal basin where waves thunder between the gaps in the rocks, churning the pool into a natural saltwater Jacuzzi. The five of us sit in the shallows, drinking beer while the water fizzes against our skin.

The holiday officially ends the next day, and I walk Queenie down the hill to the grocery store to buy yellow cake mix and chocolate frosting for Keane's birthday—his favorite flavor, according to Eamon. We sit for a few minutes on a bench outside the market, where a pair of little girls play checkers on a nearby table. They scramble from their seats when they see Queenie, and she rolls over so they can pet her belly.

"What's your dog's name?" asks the girl with yellow barrettes.

"Queenie."

They look at each other and crack up, laughing for reasons only little girls know, and the other girl, with blue baubles at the ends of her braids, says, "Is she really a queen?"

"Yes, she's the queen of the Turks and Caicos."

"If she's a queen, where's her crown?"

I drop my voice to a whisper. "She's in disguise."

Their giggles are like music.

"I like Queenie," the first girl says.

"She likes you too."

We sit like this for so long, their small brown hands tickling my dog's belly, that I can feel the strands of happiness spinning themselves, layer after layer, around Ben's memory. Creating a buffer that makes it hurt less to think about him. Someday, maybe, it won't hurt at all.

The spell is broken when the girls' mother calls them away. Queenie and I trek back up the hill to the house, where I hide my purchases in my room.

On Monday, the other sailors begin planning the passage to St. Barths. None of the particulars matter to me and I wander to my room. Begin packing for leaving. I am not ready. I'll miss my sprawling bed and the soothing nighttime peep of the coqui frogs. I'll miss the outside shower and sitting on the balcony until after the stars appear. Each island I've visited has been better than the one before, but I'm worried about St. Barths. Worried about Keane.

We leave the next evening, following our last dinner at the patchwork house, and Eamon jumps ship to sail with Agda and Felix aboard their forty-eight-foot catamaran, *Papillon*, seduced by the prospect of his own stateroom and a well-stocked bar. Keane and I have the smallest boat, so we leave first from the harbor and set sail between Jost Van Dyke and Tortola. Through the Narrows. Through Flanagan Passage. Into open water. The other boats come behind, staggering their departures so we can all reach St. Barths at about the same time. The catamaran passes us in the night. Luke and Amanda's *Fizgig*, a forty-four-foot sloop, goes by while Keane is on watch. Karoline and Jefferson are with us longer on *Peneireiro*, but eventually we end up alone.

I arrange our watch rotation so Keane is doing the first four hours on his birthday. While he is on deck, I mix the batter and slip the cake into the oven. It's still warm when I carry it up into the cockpit.

"I'd sing, but it's best for everyone involved if I don't," I say. "Happy Birthday."

Keane's eyes go wide. "You baked this for me."

"I'd use the term pretty loosely considering it baked unevenly."

"Is something wrong with the gimbal?"

"Gimbal?"

Keane laughs. "It's the mechanism that keeps the oven level under sail."

"Well," I say, handing him the cake, "that would have been a great thing to know about thirty minutes ago."

He kisses the top of my head. "You are a star, Anna. Thank you."

"A candle won't stay lit in this breeze," I say. "But I think you're still allowed to make a wish."

He squints one eye, as though considering, and nods. "Done."

We share a fork and his last bottle of Guinness as we eat the entire cake in one sitting, licking the melty chocolate frosting from our fingers. The sun is a sliver of fire on the horizon. We sit in silence, watching it rise, watching the sky turn gold.

"I think—" I turn to look at Keane. In the new morning light, his skin is as gold as the sky and the words dry up in my mouth. We look at each other too long, and his jaw twitches; he knows it too. I look away first. "I think it's going to be a good day."

"In my experience, today is usually not."

"Then you are very lucky I'm here."

Our eyes meet again. "Yes. I am."

I flee to the cabin with the excuse of needing to wash the dishes, but what I need is to escape the intensity of his gaze. Except I can't control my body's response to him. Can't slow my racing heart. Can't get beyond the thought that friends don't look at each other the way we did.

Is it too soon to want someone else? What happens to my love for Ben? Where does it go? Is this even real, or is it proximity? I sit in the cabin and try to pull myself together. Keane has gone from stranger to sailing partner to friend. Anything more could be a disaster. Or it could be really fucking incredible.

"Anna," he calls. "Come play Scrabble with me?"

"Only if you use actual words."

He laughs. "I should have bought you a Scrabble dictionary for Christmas."

The tiles are still locked in place from our last game when I unfold the board on the bench between us. "How convenient that you didn't."

"You are a sore loser."

"You cheat."

Laughing, he reaches over and pushes the bill of my Crabbers ball cap down over my face. We play Scrabble until we get hungry and Keane volunteers to make lunch. He prepares heaping turkey sandwiches and thick slices of mango from a tree back in Jost Van Dyke. I roll the ball on the foredeck for Queenie to chase, then take over while Keane snoozes in the sun. We are back to normal as we sail into night, but when the following day breaks and we get closer to the green hills and red-tiled roofs of Saint Barthélemy, Keane grows tense and quiet, and I wonder if we haven't made a mistake by coming here.

loud and defiant (24)

Gustavia is a beautiful village with tidy buildings and clean streets, and the beach off which we are anchored is covered with more seashells than anyone could count in a lifetime. Yet everything about this place feels wrong. Keane is a walking thundercloud, and as we weave our way through the New Year's Eve crowd on the Rue Jeanne d'Arc, I keep waiting for his past to ambush him.

And then it does.

"Sullivan?" A man with salt-and-pepper hair springs up from a table filled with young sailors wearing matching red crew shirts from the New Year's Eve regatta. A massive gold watch shines on his wrist, glinting when he shakes Keane's hand. "God, it's good to see you, kid. I didn't know you were in town. Were you out on the racecourse today?"

The muscle in Keane's jaw flexes, but the man misses it as he flicks the ash from his cigar onto the sidewalk. "No. We arrived this morning from Jost Van Dyke."

"Good for you, kid." The man clamps the cigar between his teeth and talks around it. "We won, so come have a victory drink."

Keane glances at me, his expression uneasy. I don't like St. Barths. The harbor and the water along the coastline are swarmed with mega-yachts owned by Russian billionaires, American politicians, and rap moguls, and I feel as out of place on this island as I did at Barbara Braithwaite's dinner table. And I don't know whether Keane is looking for an excuse to leave or permission to stay, but I am not the boss. I shrug. "Why not?"

Over glasses of ti' punch that are terrible and strong, I am introduced to Jackson Kemp, the founder of the biggest waste management company in the United States, and the owner of the boat Keane sailed aboard five years ago. The same man whose email rejection in Nassau pushed Keane into a drunken binge.

"You're looking great, kid." Jackson claps him on the shoulder. "They're doing amazing things with prosthetics these days. Almost as good as the real thing."

The dismissive way he calls Keane "kid" crawls up my spine and settles between my shoulders. I don't like this man or his careless language. Keane shoves a hand up through his hair and I don't understand why he would continue doing something that causes him so much pain . . . until I realize I do understand.

"Shame they haven't found a way to replace insensitive assholes yet." I mutter it into my drink, but apparently loud enough for Jackson Kemp to hear. Keane blinks at me as if I am someone he's never seen before—and right now I am. Jackson's eyes widen, and he unleashes a booming laugh.

"Guess I deserved that."

"I guess."

"Listen, I'm throwing a party tonight at my villa. Y'all should come." He looks from me to Keane and back, offering what might be as close to an apology as Keane is going to get. "The champagne will be flowing, and we'll have a prime view of the fireworks."

I set my drink down on the table and look at Keane. "I just remembered there's somewhere I need to be."

"Anna, wait." I hear his voice behind me, but I don't turn around. He catches up to me before I've made it to the end of the sidewalk. "Where are you going?"

I wheel around to face him. "I don't know, *kid*. Maybe I'll sail to Saint Kitts or Nevis. Anywhere is better than here. You can stay if you want, but I have no interest in anyone who doesn't recognize you for the exceptional human being you are."

Standing in the middle of the sidewalk, he circles his arms around my shoulders and draws me to him. I slip my arms around his waist and press my cheek against his soft shirt. "You deserve so much better than this. Come with me."

He exhales into my hair and kisses the top of my head. "Let's go."

Together we walk down the Rue de la Plage to Shell Beach and motor the dinghy out to where the four boats are rafted together in the small harbor. Eamon is playing poker with the other guys on *Fizgig*—Queenie sitting beside him as if she's learning how to play—while the women sunbathe topless on *Papillon*'s trampoline. Keane crosses from one boat to the next to speak with his brother, while I take off the sail covers and secure our gear. I'm in the cabin when Eamon comes belowdecks.

"Anna." He pulls me into a hug. One of my favorite things about Sullivan men is how unreserved they are with their affections. "Thank you for letting me sail with you. It's been grand."

"You're not coming with us?"

"My holiday is nearly over, so I'll fly out from here in a day or two."

"Thank you for the autopilot."

"Thank you for looking after my brother," he says. "I know you think he's helping you, but I reckon it's the other way around."

When we're ready to go, Eamon helps us detach from *Peneireiro* and hands me the dock lines. "Fair winds, Anna. I hope we'll meet again one day."

"Me too. Have a safe trip home."

We motor through the field of boats anchored off St. Barths. One of the mega-yachts we pass is at least five hundred feet long and has a black hull so shiny, I can see my boat reflected. Tonight that boat will be filled with beautiful people drinking champagne as fireworks burst over their heads. Maybe Keane and I will be able to see the fireworks from wherever we are when the New Year arrives. But once we reach the open water and raise the sails, I find I don't care about fireworks at all.

"Where should we go?" I sit beside Keane in the cockpit. He's wearing his favorite shirt—the one he was wearing the first time I saw him—and a smile that makes it impossible for me not to smile back. I can't see his eyes behind his sunglasses, but the stress lines between his eyebrows have faded away.

"I'd like to take you to my favorite island in the whole Caribbean."

"And where would that be?"

"It's a surprise."

There are at least half a dozen islands within easy sailing distance of St. Barths and I could probably figure it out if I tried, but he is happy and we are at sea. "Okay."

After Ben died, I imagined my life proceeding in shades of gray, but tonight, as the sun sinks below the ocean, the sky and sea are purple. Queenie presses her warm body against my thigh and my brain pushes against the guilty feeling that it's too soon. That I'm not allowed to be this happy yet. I lean my head back, my face tilted up to the sky, and I say the words, loud and defiant. "I am so fucking happy right now."

"I've never been so glad to put a place behind me," he says. "I thought going to Saint Barths might . . ."

"Exorcise the demons," I finish. "I understand too well how that doesn't work."

The tension falls out of his shoulders. "I've never told anyone except my parents, but the person driving the Mercedes that night was an American senator."

"Are you serious?"

Keane nods. "He keeps getting reelected by championing family values, but on that particular New Year's Eve, he was drunk, his mistress sitting in the passenger's seat. Now, whenever I need a new prosthesis, I send the bill to a Washington, D.C., post office box and the bill gets paid. As long as I keep his identity a secret, I'm set for life."

"Are you ever tempted to go public?"

"Sometimes," he says. "But I have the best prosthetics the senator's money can buy and he has to live with his hypocrisy."

"Do you really think he does?" I ask.

"Perhaps not, but karma will catch up to him one day," Keane says. "Anyway, it was pretty fucking spectacular hearing you call Jackson Kemp an arse. I don't imagine he's used to anyone being bold enough to try that—at least not to his face."

"I wanted to punch him but figured calling him an asshole would be slightly more polite," I say. "I'm sorry if I ruined your relationship with him. Listening to him talk was painful."

"I'm sorry I dragged you through my mess."

"Your mess. My mess. At this point I feel like we're in this together."

"It's strange letting go of something that's played such an enormous role in my life," Keane says. "Not sure what to do now."

"What about the Paralympics?"

"There's a guy who's been after me to get my citizenship and join the US team, but I've always felt like it would be admitting I'm not capable of racing against able sailors," he says. "Which is an ableist thing to believe, but that's the ugly truth of it."

"Okay, so . . . what if you assembled a team of sailors with disabilities and compete against able crews?" I suggest. "If you can't join them, beat them."

He regards me silently before the corner of his mouth kicks up in a wry grin. "I'd need a boat."

"So we'll get sponsors."

"We?"

"Do you think I trust you to do this by yourself?" I say. "Besides, you'll need someone to handle the operations while you're off racing—and I don't have a job."

Keane laughs. "I'll need three references and a letter of recommendation."

"Can I use your brother as a reference?"

"Not if you want the job."

"The first person you should probably contact is Jackson Kemp," I say. "A little guilt money to get things started."

This could all be for nothing, but talking keeps our minds off an unknown future, gives us something to plan, and late into the night we discuss building a nonprofit organization. And when the clock strikes the end of the year, Keane and I have filled his little notebook with possibilities.

To the west, fireworks paint the distant sky, which rules out St. Kitts as a destination. Maybe Keane is taking us to Nevis. Maybe Antigua or Guadeloupe or Dominica. It doesn't really matter, because we're together.

"It's midnight." He says the words as I'm thinking them, and my stomach twists itself into a knot. "Happy New Year, Anna."

"Happy New Year."

He kisses my forehead with his eyes closed, as if he can find the way without a map. His lips are feather-soft, and then gone. He touches my face, trailing his thumb from the corner of my mouth to a spot just below my ear, and tiny earthquakes explode in its wake. His eyes are open now, met with mine, and I can hardly breathe because what happens next will change everything. I am not in love with Keane Sullivan, but I could be. All it would take is accepting the heart he wears on his sleeve and promising not to break it. He leans in, his smile a spark that sets my nerve endings on fire.

And he is kissing me.

Slowly.

His fingers never leave my face.

There is no frantic clutching of clothes. No wild clash of tongues. This is not kissing as a precursor; this is him kissing me as if I am first, last, and everything in between. It feels so damn good, I can't help but smile and his reply is a soft laugh that I catch in my mouth. The line between love and not-love is so very thin. Minutes pass. Hours. Decades. Lifetimes. His lips come away slowly, then he kisses the top of my nose and shifts his arm so I can tuck up against him. It's not so very different from the way we always sit, except my mouth is filled with sweetness. His fingers move gently in my hair. And my heart is beating *him, him, him.*

"That was . . ." I trail off, unable to find the right word amid the thoughts piling up in my brain. I kissed Ben so many times, but kissing Keane is somehow . . . better. I don't know how to process that.

"Better than calling Jackson Kemp an arse?"

I laugh, grateful for the way Keane always seems to know how to defuse the emotional bombs in my head. "Almost."

"So, you know, I wasn't plotting it," he says. "But the opportunity arose, and you didn't seem to mind, so I—"

"Stop talking."

This time I kiss him, giving in to the pleasure of sinking my fingers into the softness of his hair. Paying attention to the sounds that teach me what he likes. I am not ready for more than this—not yet—but this is good. It is enough.

today is a doorway (25)

I wake when the sun comes through the open hatch in the V-berth and I hear the soft slap of water against a hull that isn't sailing. Through the companionway I see Keane on deck, making up lines. Wherever we were going in the night, we've arrived. I climb out of bed and slip into the bathroom to brush my teeth because kissing him has become a distinct possibility and I don't want morning breath. When I finish, he's in the cabin, about to start brewing a pot of coffee.

"Good morning," he says.

"Hi." My cheeks are warm. I feel shy and I wonder if I'm the only one who can feel the undercurrent of bashfulness. "Did you sail all night?"

The cabin feels smaller than ever as I move toward him, not knowing how this works. Are we more than friends today? Or was last night a New Year's Eve one-off?

"I did," Keane says. "I had enough energy last night to power a city."

"Thanks for letting me sleep."

He reaches out, hands gentle on my hips as he pulls me in. My arms fit up around his neck and when our lips come together, there's a hint of toothpaste in his mouth too. The first kiss is tentative and soft. In the space before the next kiss—no more than a heartbeat—need crashes over me like a wave. My hips roll against him and his hands move lower, pressing me closer until it's hard to tell where I end and he begins. Unlike last night, today is a doorway. We just have to step through.

"Is this going to ruin us?" I'm breathless as I ask.

"No." He kisses my neck, sending a rash of shivers down my back. I shudder and his laugh is wicked and delicious.

"Are you sure?"

"I have been a sure thing since Bimini, Anna." He touches his forehead to mine. "When you looked at me and said 'I've changed my mind about those eggs,' your face was frightened and fierce, and right then I knew I'd follow you to the ends of the earth if you'd let me."

"I don't think I really had a lightning bolt moment," I say. Keane stepped into my world a stranger and quietly became someone so necessary that I don't want to be without him.

"Doesn't matter," he says. "We've arrived at the same place."

"Where exactly are we?"

He laughs. "Go on. Have a look."

I climb out on deck to find us anchored in a small bay on a volcanic island where thick clouds are gathered at the top of the tallest hill. "Is this . . . Montserrat?"

"It is."

When Ben and I planned our trip, guidebooks made little mention of the island, aside from the Soufrière Hills volcano eruption in 1995 that buried most of the island under lava and ash. Even cruisers on internet sailing forums recommended the island only as an overnight anchorage while en route to more southerly destinations. Ben wanted to see this island more than any other, but I keep that to myself. If this is Keane's favorite place, I want to see it through his eyes.

* * *

"Montserrat reminds me most of home," he says as we run the dinghy to the town dock at Little Bay, although *town* is a generous word for a handful of buildings. "The cliffs and green hills are very much like Ireland, and a good many of the people, regardless of skin color, are of Irish descent."

"It's prettier than I expected."

"Not an uncommon reaction," he says. "People expect to see only devastation, but there's so much beauty here. Just wait."

The lady at the customs office checks our clearance papers from Jost Van Dyke—we pretend like St. Barths never happened—and we pay the necessary port fees. In the same building is immigration, where our passports are stamped, and we have officially arrived on Montserrat. We come out from the warehouse and a police car pulls up alongside the building. A brown-skinned officer wearing a crisp white uniform shirt steps out of the car and says to Keane, "Top of the morning."

"May the road rise up to meet you," Keane replies, his accent exaggerated. The corner of his mouth twitches as if he wants to laugh, but I have no idea what's happening.

"And may you arrive in heaven before the devil knows you're dead," the officer says, his attempt at an Irish accent mangled by his Montserratian tongue, and the two break into laughter, pulling each other in for a hug.

"Anna." Keane slips an arm around my waist. "This is my great friend and quite possibly sixth cousin once removed on my father's side, Desmond Sullivan. Desmond, this is Anna Beck, my partner in crime."

Keane skillfully sidesteps giving our relationship a definition, a relief because it feels too new for that. I shake hands with Desmond, and he leads us over to his patrol car.

"My shift won't be ending until midafternoon," he says. "But I can drive you up to my house until I'm finished."

"There's a small matter of a dog," Keane says. "A pot hound we adopted in the Turks and Caicos. She's got all her inoculations and proper papers, but I understand there's a necessary permit?"

"Bring her ashore," Desmond says with a wink. "If anyone asks, she's mine."

"You sneaky bastard."

Desmond laughs. "Runs in the family."

Keane and I go out to the sailboat for Queenie and our bags, and return to Little Bay Beach, where we drag the dinghy above the tide line and tie it to a tree. Queenie does fishtail slides in the black sand, happy for freedom after so many hours on the boat. When she's finally settled, panting and smiling, we clip her to the leash and head up to the road, where Desmond is waiting.

"The Montserrat Festival comes to a close today," he says,

driving us along narrow hilly roads lined with trees and ferns. Everything is so green. "Sharon and Miles will be at the parade, but when we are all home, we'll have a proper lime, yeah?"

"That would be grand," Keane says, and explains to me that "having a lime" means hanging out with friends, eating, drinking, talking, listening to music. "In Ireland we call it *craic*"—he pronounces it like *crack*—"but the concept is the same."

Desmond lives in a village called Lookout. His little mango-yellow house sits on a hill overlooking a bay where the water is the same shade as the blue shutters framing the windows.

"Lookout," he says, letting us in through the red front door, "was built after the volcano destroyed the lower part of the island and many people relocated here. It doesn't have a rich history yet, so it's still discovering its flavor."

He leaves us with an invitation to make ourselves at home, but there are only two bedrooms.

"We can't kick Miles out of his room," I say. "Even if Desmond insists."

"I agree, which is why I packed the tent."

"You think of everything."

He catches me around the waist with one hand and reels me in. "Care to guess what I'm thinking now?"

"That you need a shower?"

One hand against my neck, his thumb on my cheek, he kisses me softly. Then deeply. I run my palms up the back of his T-shirt and we kiss there in the kitchen until we're breathless.

"A cold shower," he says. "Most definitely cold."

While Keane is showering, I wash out the liner for his prosthesis. I've never done it before, but I've watched enough to know how to do it. His everyday prosthesis stands beside the bathtub, so I leave a clean liner and a sock draped over the socket and sit down on the closed toilet seat lid. "Is this whole thing as scary for you as it is for me?"

"Us, you mean?" he says from behind the floral curtain.

"Yeah."

"Not even a bit."

"I guess, after Ben, I'm afraid of having the rug pulled out from under me again."

"Which makes absolute sense," Keane says. "Ben was suffering from something over which he had little control, but I've been to that same dark place and I made a different choice. That doesn't mean I don't have bleak days when I hate myself and everyone else. But if I can promise you nothing else, it's that I intend to leave this world old, stooped, and with white hairs sticking out of my ears. And if having that image pressed into your brain hasn't given you second thoughts, well . . . I'm yours for as long as you want me."

For so long I thought that falling for someone else would mean I didn't love Ben enough. That what we had wasn't real. I haven't stopped loving him. I just don't want to regret letting Keane Sullivan go. "You might be stuck with me awhile."

"I never saw myself having this conversation in a bathroom on Montserrat." The water cuts off and his face appears around the edge of the shower curtain. "But the longer I'm stuck with you, the better."

* * *

Within walking distance, we find a small food hut beside the road, where we sit on plastic chairs and eat roti stuffed with potatoes and gravy that we wash down with cold Carib beer. We play a game guessing the color of the next car to come down the road, then slowly walk back to Desmond's house, waving whenever the locals greet us.

Desmond is home when we arrive. A moment later Sharon comes into the house, her arms laden with grocery bags. She is a tall woman with natural curls who thanks me when I take a few of the bags. Miles, maybe in kindergarten, is missing a front tooth.

"Miles." Desmond squats down beside his son. "This is my friend Keane Sullivan."

The little boy's eyes go wide. "Sullivan like me?"

"Yes."

"I can spell Sullivan," Miles announces. He calls out the letters in the correct order, raising a finger with each one until he's holding up eight. "Eight letters."

"That's very good," Keane says. "I only just learned how to spell Sullivan properly."

Miles cracks up laughing. "Maybe I'm smarter than you."

"I reckon so."

"Keane," Sharon says, hugging him with one arm and kissing his cheek. "It's about time you showed up. We've missed you."

"Likewise," he says. "Sharon, this is Anna Beck, my plus-one."

"He lies," I say, following her to the kitchen. "He's my plus-one."

As I place the groceries onto the kitchen counter facing the living room, Miles broaches the subject of Keane's leg, his little voice almost a whisper when he asks, "Are you like Iron Man?"

"A bit," Keane says. "Only the one leg, though."

"Cool."

Satisfied that his father's friend is superhero adjacent, Miles runs outside to play. Desmond and Keane step out to the side porch with bottles of Guinness—"the proper beverage for liming"—while I help Sharon unpack.

"How long have you been together?" she asks.

"We've been sailing together for a little more than a month," I say. "But we've been together for about . . . sixteen hours."

Sharon laughs. "That's very specific."

"It took some time for us—for me, actually—to figure things out."

"He's a good man." She takes a couple more bottles of Guinness from the refrigerator, opens them, and hands one to me. "Let's go outside. We've got people coming over after the festival, so we'll worry about the food later."

The four of us sit on chairs overlooking Margarita Bay while Miles turns somersaults in the grass and plays with Queenie. Desmond tells me how, seven years ago, he met a drunken Keane urinating along the side of the road. "I was going to arrest him, but when he said his name was Sullivan, I brought him home and sobered him up."

"What he's not telling you," Keane says, "is that after he got me sober, he took me out for goat stew and Guinness, and we got drunk all over again."

Sharon tells me she's a stylist in a hair salon in the neighboring village of St. John's, and when she asks me what I do for a living, I don't mention the pirate bar. I share our plan to start a nonprofit organization. I feel embarrassed by how privileged it is to want to raise money for a high-tech sailboat when Montserrat has been rebuilding for more than two decades, but her smile is generous. "That would be good for him. He needs a purpose."

As afternoon turns into evening, friends and family trickle in, including a girl dressed in a hot-pink gown with a sparkling tiara on her head and a Miss Montserrat sash draped over her shoulder. She is Sharon's sister, Tanice, straight from the festival.

"You needn't have brought out the royalty on our account," Keane says. "We're regular folk."

Sharon straightens her shoulders and gives a small head toss. "But I am no regular folk, Mr. Sullivan. I am sister to the queen."

Tanice rolls her eyes and goes for Desmond's CD collection to put on music, removing her tiara and kicking off her high heels. A group of men start barbecuing chicken on the grill, and some of the women come inside to unwrap their potluck side dishes. I wander between the two groups, Guinness in hand, listening to them lament about how long it's taken to turn Little Bay into a proper town and catching snippets of gossip about people I don't know.

I walk around to the west side of the house to watch the sun go down. Keane comes up behind me, slips his arms around my shoulders, and rests his chin on top of my head. "If you keep your eyes just above the sun as it slips below the horizon, you may see the green flash."

We watch together and I try not to blink, but as the sun sinks, I see nothing but sky. "I missed it."

"Next time, then," Keane says, kissing my cheek. "We've got many sunsets to come."

the real world (26)

Sharon drops us off in the village of St. Peter's the next morning at the Fogarty Hill end of the Oriole Walkway, a trail that runs through the island's center hills to Lawyers Mountain. Queenie stays behind to play with Miles, while Keane and I go hiking in a dense forest of trees, roped with vines bearing leaves as big as our heads, and ferns growing thick along the trail. Keane points out a large iguana crawling through the branches of a tree and we hear—but don't see—the croak of mountain chickens, a once abundant frog, endangered since the eruptions.

The climb is steeper than we anticipated and when we reach the summit, our shirts are damp with sweat. But at an elevation of more than 1,200 feet, we can see in every direction. To the north, my boat is a blue dot in Little Bay. Beyond it are the Silver Hills, remnants of a dead volcano. In the south, clouds of steam and gas hover above the dome of the quiet Soufrière Hills volcano and the pyroclastic flow cuts across the green island like an angry gray scar. Nevis and Antigua are rocky blue shadows on the horizon.

"After listening to the talk last night about unfinished construction and unfulfilled campaign promises, I don't know how the island sustains itself," I say. "But up here, I understand why people wouldn't want to leave. I understand why you love it."

"So many people are attracted to the wreckage," Keane says. "But the people are the reason I come back."

On our way down the mountainside, we fill our pockets with lemons and guavas from trees along the trail. When we reach the end, Sharon and Miles are waiting. Queenie watches us approach from the open back window of the little SUV, her tail a furious blur.

"If it wouldn't be a bother, would you mind dropping us at Little Bay so we can check on the boat?" Keane says. "We'll call a taxi to bring us to Lookout, so you won't have to come fetch us."

Sharon leaves us at Little Bay and Queenie jumps into the dinghy before we've pushed it off the beach. On the boat, we check the bilge, make sure the engine starts, and then collapse in the shade of the cockpit tent. Keane removes his prosthesis, sock, and liner, and rubs the back of his residual limb. He didn't complain of pain during the hike, but he looks uncomfortable.

"Can I do that for you?"

"What? Rub my leg?"

"It always feels better when someone else does it."

"It does." His eyes meet mine and hold there. "But you don't have to do it."

"I want to."

I lean forward and take the lower part of his right leg in my hands. His limb is a topographical map, raised ridges of scars and soft valleys of normal skin, and touching him this way feels almost too intimate. But when I work my fingertips gently against the muscles along the back of his leg, he closes his eyes and sighs. I knead my thumbs along the back of his knee and his groan is pure pleasure. "Jesus, that feels good."

It doesn't take long for my fingers to feel comfortable with the scar patterns on his skin, for it to stop feeling foreign and start feeling like Keane. His eyes are still closed when I notice a rise in the front of his shorts.

His eyes fly open.

"Fuck. Anna, I'm sorry, I—" He scrubs a hand over his face while he covers the front of his shorts with the other. "It doesn't mean anything. It's—That's not true. I want you so badly right now, I can barely stand it."

It's been almost a year since the last time I had sex. My body has been ready, but my brain is the reluctant sex organ. I think too much. Worry it's too soon.

"I crave you all the time," Keane says. "I've imagined you naked more than once when I was—well, when I was alone with my thoughts, but—"

"Oh my God." I laugh, my face growing warm. "How can I possibly compete with the fantasy?"

"Come here." He extends a hand and I let him draw me onto his lap, facing him. Through the layers of fabric between us, I can feel his arousal pressing against me. His hands are big and warm on my back as he kisses me, his lips salty from sweat. "I can promise you that nothing I've imagined could ever be better than the real thing. You are the fantasy."

"I'm starting to think you're too good to be true. No one is this perfect."

"In case you haven't noticed, I'm missing a leg and I'm unemployed, so you could probably do better."

"Probably." The scruff on his jaw is soft beneath my palms when I take his face in my hands. "But for some reason, I want you too."

My mouth is on his when Queenie squirms between us, reminding us that we are not entirely alone. I'm slightly disappointed, slightly relieved. "I think your other girl also needs some attention."

Keane scratches her behind the ears as he looks at me. "Would you mind if we press pause on this moment?"

"We have all the time in the world," I say. "Maybe we should go swimming instead."

Our bathing suits are back at the house, so we peel down to our underwear and leap off the boat. The dog barks at us.

"Queenie, jump." I gesture for her to come into the water and her feet dance with excitement. She walks back and forth along the deck, barking as if that will bring us back out of the water. Finally she leaps. She hits the surface with an ungainly pelican splash, but paddles to me and then to Keane.

We swim to shore, where he sits at the water's edge while Queenie and I chase each other up and down the empty beach, displacing the seabirds who swoop and cry for us to go away. When I give up the game, Queenie brings Keane a bit of driftwood that he throws into the water for her to fetch.

"This trip has spoiled me for dry land." I drop down onto the sand beside him. "I don't want to go back to the real world."

He laughs. "You're in the real world, Anna."

"You know what I mean."

"I do," he says. "But people opt out of a nine-to-five existence all the time. If you want to keep sailing, you'll find a way. Or you can return to Florida and live aboard the boat. Whatever works for you."

"What about you?"

"Wherever you are is where I want to be."

"And the wind gods?"

He flings the stick. "Can go fuck themselves."

I lie back on the sand, smiling. Allowing myself to imagine Keane and me living aboard the Alberg together. "It's a pretty small boat for two people and a dog."

"It'll do for now."

Once the boat is secure, we call for a cab. My underwear is damp beneath my clothes and my face pink from the sun as Keane pays the taxi driver in front of Desmond's house. Sharon tends to a small yellow frangipani tree in the front yard and Queenie races straight to Miles, who is kicking a soccer ball. Although I loved the outdoor shower in Jost Van Dyke, there is comfort in the way Miles's toys are tucked into the corners of the bathtub as I'm showering off sand and salt.

Desmond returns from work and drives us all to the exclusion zone in the southern part of the island. On the way, he explains that travel in Zone V—the area around the volcano where the worst of the damage occurred—is limited to scientists from the Montserrat Volcano Observatory and law enforcement. Areas farther from the volcano are open for daytime access to tour groups, island visitors, and farmers whose livestock still roams in the exclusion zone.

We are waved through the police checkpoint and Desmond drives along the ash-filled bed of the Belham River. Soon we start seeing the abandoned houses. Some look as if they could still have people living inside, while others have broken windows and weeds creeping from the outside in. Deeper into the zone, we pass a house that was flooded with mud and ash, leaving only the second floor exposed. We drive along a golf course rendered unrecognizable by lava rock and ash.

"My parents' house in Plymouth was completely destroyed," Sharon says. "It's one thing to move away from your childhood home, but another thing entirely for that home to no longer exist. Sometimes I'm sad that I cannot show Miles where I lived when I was a little girl, and he will never know a Granny and Gramps who haven't lived in Saint John's, but it does no good to dwell in the past."

Plymouth is a ghost town trapped in a river of rock, and the neighboring towns of Richmond Hill and Kinsale are filled with crumbling homes like broken, abandoned seashells. Over it all looms the ash cloud, dark and sulfuric.

"The volcano has been quiet," Desmond says. "But every day there is seismic activity, tiny earthquakes that tell scientists the island is alive."

Plymouth is not a tomb, but we are solemn on the ride back to Lookout. Miles chatters softly to Queenie as if she understands him, but there is nothing meaningful Keane or I could say about the volcano that probably hasn't already been said. By the time we reach the house, dinner—curried goat and potatoes stewed in Sharon's Crock-Pot—is ready. Guinness, leftover from last night's party, cuts through our quiet and Desmond asks how Keane and I met.

As we share the story, Keane brings up *Chemineau* and, to my horror, starts talking about Sara. I can't imagine he would be so insensitive as to talk about having sex with her, but he's also honest to a fault.

"That night ranks as one of the worst of my life," he says. "I suffered from performance anxiety because I was utterly smitten with Anna, but the final straw was when I called Sara by Anna's name. None of you will be surprised that Sara kicked me off the boat and I did not, in fact, sleep with her."

"Actually, I'm surprised," I say. "When you went to confession the next day—"

"I didn't go to confession."

"Liar."

"Listen, I was simply asking the deacon his professional opinion on whether what happened with Sara—or didn't happen, as the case may be—might be a sin," he says. "He told me my judgment probably wasn't the most sound but gave me an unofficial blessing to be sure, and here we are."

Sharon covers her smile with her hand, but Desmond laughs so hard that tears trickle from the corners of his eyes.

"The whole incident might have been avoided if I'd told Anna how I felt at the time," Keane goes on. "But given we'd only known each other one week, she'd have thought me mad."

"How would that be different from now?" I ask.

He winks. "Because now you're stuck with me."

The rest of our story gets lost in laughter and Sharon telling us how she was my age when she met Desmond during the Montserrat Festival, where he was competing in the Calypso Monarch singing contest. "He was a terrible singer," she says. "But so cute, I didn't have the heart to tell him."

"It's the Sullivan charm," Desmond says. "Once you are hooked, there's no escaping it."

true affection (27)

Sunday feels like a leaving day.

Desmond takes us to the dive shop in Little Bay, where Keane rents a tank and spends the morning scraping barnacles from the bottom of the boat. I clean the cabin and send Happy New Year emails home, telling my mom and Carla that we are on Montserrat. But I'm not ready to share my relationship with Keane yet. It's too new and I want to hold on to the secret a little longer. Together we take stock of our supplies, but since we've had most of our meals with the Sullivans or on-island, we buy only a twelve-pack of Coke and some fresh fruits.

"We should go soon." Keane gives voice to what I've been thinking as we return the dive gear to the shop. "Desmond and Sharon would have us stay as long as we like, but I fear wearing out our welcome."

"What's next?"

"Guadeloupe, Dominica, and Martinique are all about a day's sail apart from one another, and the weather will be with us," he says. "We can visit any or all of them. It's up to you."

I don't even consider Ben's route anymore. We've blown past islands he wanted to visit and been to places that weren't part of his plan. The only thing I regret is not helping to do the research so I would know what each island has to offer.

"What would you choose?" I ask Keane.

"Martinique is my next favorite place in the Caribbean," he says. "I'd drop anchor for the night in both Guadeloupe and Dominica and go ashore at Martinique."

"Let's do that."

We take a taxi to the house to gather our things and say goodbye to Sharon and Miles, promising we'll return to Montserrat soon. Miles hugs Queenie until she wriggles away. At the harbor, we're loading the dinghy with our gear when Desmond's patrol car drives up and he gets out. I wait for him to play the Irish cliché game with Keane, but instead Desmond only says, "I wish you could stay a bit longer."

"We could," Keane says. "But Miles has to go back to school and Sharon to work, and we don't want to become an imposition. Best remember us with fondness."

"That would assume I'm fond of you."

"Kiss my arse, Sullivan."

Desmond grins and pulls Keane into a hug. "Farewell, my friend. Come back to us soon. And, Anna"—it's my turn for a hug—"you are always welcome in our home."

He watches from the dock as we pull anchor and motor away. He is a blur in my eyes as I wave goodbye.

* * *

We sail from Montserrat to Guadeloupe, where we anchor in the harbor at Deshaies. Eat. Sleep. Wake up in the morning and sail to Dominica. We spend the night in Prince Rupert Bay. Eat. Sleep. Sail. On our way to Martinique, I try my hand at fishing and land a small blackfin tuna that we eat for lunch, seared, with homemade guava salsa. As Keane predicted, the wind has been in our favor, and the only difference between these crossings and previous easy hops is that we spend less time arguing over Scrabble and more time kissing. We've slept together in the V-berth but haven't had sex. At first I appreciated Keane's patience as I got used to the idea of having an intimate connection with someone other than Ben. But . . . we've waited long enough.

In Martinique, we anchor in a harbor that looks like a postcard come to life. Where turquoise ocean touches white sand beside the red-roofed village and green mountains behind. The hills surrounding the bay are a welcoming hug and the wooden jetty appears to come straight out from the front door of the village church.

"Welcome to Les Anses d'Arlet," Keane says. "The best place on earth."

"Wait. I thought Montserrat was your favorite."

"Taken as a whole, it is," he says. "But I could easily live out the rest of my days in this village."

"Well, my expectations suddenly got higher."

I take the dinghy to shore and use a computer in a restaurant to clear through customs. While I have Wi-Fi, I rent a guesthouse up the hill from the beach. When I go back to the boat for Keane and Queenie, I tell him to pack an overnight bag. "I have a surprise for you."

"As good as Puerto Rican baseball?" he asks.

"Better."

Fifteen minutes and a steep hill later, we arrive at a small wooden cottage with an outdoor kitchen and a view of the harbor. A striped hammock big enough for two is hanging on the veranda, but the focal point of the room is the large bed with fresh white bedding and a mosquito net draped along the headboard.

Keane takes it all in, and nods. "This is most certainly going to be better than baseball."

I laugh, shutting Queenie in the bathroom with food, water, and her favorite tennis ball. "Definitely. I mean, I figured we could go to the beach or hiking in the forest or—"

He stops me with soft kisses, one after another, a hand sliding into my hair as the other seeks out the hollow of my lower back. Soft becomes harder, more urgent, and I clutch the back of his T-shirt in my fists, my heart thumping a wild beat. It may be that I push him backward or he draws me forward, but together we find the edge of the bed. He sits and pulls me onto his lap.

He touches my cheek. "Are you ready for me, Anna?"

"Yes," I whisper, turning to brush my lips against the inside of his wrist. "Yes."

He works open the buttons of my shirt. Keane has seen me in my bikini and the other day in my wet pink polka-dot bra, but today I feel exposed. The glue has only just dried on my broken heart and I'm offering him a hammer. But when he kisses my skin, just there, above my heart, I feel safe.

My shirt lands on the floor as he kisses my shoulder. I tug his shirt up over his head and send it to the ground. Kiss the corner of his mouth that always lifts first whenever he grins. I stand to remove my shorts, and Keane watches as I unclasp the front of my bra and take off my underwear. I worry that my breasts are too small and my pubic hair too much, but when I hear his sharp intake of breath and my name on the exhale, I'm reassured. Need settles heavy between my thighs.

Feeling bolder, I straddle him again and follow as he moves backward on the bed, first beneath me, then above me. The sheets press cool against my back as his mouth forges a warm trail down my body. Insecurity creeps in as I feel his mouth on my inner thigh, but it's lost to the pleasure of his tongue.

My legs are still trembling with release when he removes his prosthesis and his shorts and slips on a condom. He moves over me. Inside me. "Oh my God." I groan into his shoulder. "You have no idea how good this feels."

Keane rolls his eyes and shifts his hips, making me gasp. "Yeah, none at all."

At first we're laughing and out of sync—two bodies that have never moved together before—but once we find our rhythm, the world around us disappears. And when it's over, our skin damp and our breath short, the words repeat in my head like a litany. *I love you. I love you. I love you.* I'm afraid to say them, but when I kiss them silently into his mouth, it feels as if he's giving them right back to me.

"Jesus, Anna, that was—" He blows out a breath and presses his lips to my forehead. As much as I love the feel of his mouth

on mine, forehead kisses are the Sullivan sign of true affection
and they are my favorite.

"Exactly."

He laughs, rolling off me, and raises his arm for me to fit up
against him. "I reckon you've ruined me now."

"I'm not even sorry."

As we lie together, the sun casts a square on the floor, and
outside, the birds squawk. A tiny green gecko scurries up the wall
beside the bed, lingering to stare at us. I focus on these things.
On Queenie's short, sharp bark that demands freedom. On the
steady beat of Keane's heart beneath my ear. Anything to hold at
bay the guilt that my feelings for this man might be bigger than
anything I've ever known.

* * *

There are a lot of things we could be doing in Martinique, but
the first three days we spend nearly all our time in bed, ventur-
ing out only to take Queenie for a walk or eat in the open-air
kitchen. I cut Keane's hair using a pair of scissors I found in a
drawer, and he shows me his self-care routine, explaining the layers and how he maintains his prostheses. We memorize each other's bodies like maps, learning the places to avoid and the places
to linger. We sleep. Make love. Talk. Fuck. Laugh. The time is
a crash course in being together—although we've been learning
since the beginning—and we go back to the Alberg with everything we've discovered.

The cabin of the boat smells like the oranges hanging in
the mesh bag above the galley, and I smile at the sight of my

Cangrejeros hat hanging on its hook beside the companionway. The blue is already beginning to fade in the sun, and it has molded to the shape of my head. The Pig Beach starfish stand in a row on the ledge in the V-berth. The photo of Keane and me at the patchwork house hangs beside the photo of Ben and me. A new house rising up beside the old.

"I've hung the hammock," Keane says, coming into the cabin as I'm making up the bed. He slips his arms around my waist from behind. "But sleeping naked beneath this fluffy duvet with you is going to be the best part."

Warmth rises in my cheeks, even though we've been more naked than clothed over the past two days, and he laughs softly.

"I have a gift for you." He rummages through his duffel. "I bought this in San Juan and then you gave me Ben's mug, and I feared it was too much and not enough, but now . . . here."

He thrusts a palm-size package at me, done up in Christmas wrapping. While I tear open the paper, Keane rubs a hand across the top of his head. He's nervous. So I'm nervous too.

Inside is a pair of earrings with raw, unpolished stones set in sterling silver.

"They're rough diamonds," he says. "Conflict free. I saw them in a shop window in Old Town and they were just . . . you."

"They're beautiful."

"Like I said."

I laugh as I kiss him. "Could you be less smooth once in a while?"

"I love you," he blurts out. "And I know I should have kept that to myself a bit longer, but it's the truth and I am feeling particularly un-smooth at the moment."

"I . . . don't know how to respond to that."

"Not exactly what I'd hoped you'd say, but—"

"No, I mean . . . I'm scared. Ready to love you, but also not. I still think about Ben sometimes and I don't know how to stop doing that. And maybe this will blow up in our faces but . . . I want to try." My shoulders sag. "That was the least romantic declaration ever."

Keane nods a little. "I wouldn't put it on a greeting card."

"I love you too." The words come out on the back of a breath and the beginning of a smile. I didn't mean to say them out loud, but here they are. "I don't want you to be a rebound thing, Keane Sullivan. I want you to be the real thing."

He holds my face lightly, tenderly, and kisses me. "Count on it."

* * *

The next morning we take a series of buses to Fort-de-France, where we rent a car. As we head back south, Keane won't tell me where we're going, only that there is something he wants me to see. At the top of a bluff overlooking the ocean, near the town of Le Diamant, he brings me to a cluster of twenty concrete statues arranged in the shape of a triangle.

"In 1830, after slavery had been abolished in the islands," Keane says, "a trader ship was bringing a secret cargo of slaves to Martinique. The ship was improperly anchored in the harbor and crashed into Diamond Rock"—he points to a lone rock jutting out of the sea—"drowning forty slaves, shackled together and chained to the hold."

There is a defeated stoop to the shoulders of the statues, their brows carved heavy with sadness and their mouths turned down.

They stand in a grassy field above the vast blue of the ocean, frozen in mourning, their sorrow eternal, and tears fill my eyes.

"The statues were arranged to symbolize the triangular trade route from West Africa to the Caribbean to the American colonies," Keane says. "And they point a hundred and ten degrees toward the Gulf of Guinea. Toward home."

I'm crying in earnest now.

"We build memorials to honor the memory of those we've lost, and to remember the tragedy of humans treating other humans as property," he says. "I've been considering what you said about not knowing how to stop thinking about Ben and—well, I'd never ask that. You've already built a place for him in your heart, but if you've got a bit of room to spare . . ."

My face is wet, tears clinging to my lips, when I kiss him and whisper, "There is so much room for you."

Back at Les Anses d'Arlet, we spend the afternoon sitting at a plastic table under a party tent, drinking Lorraines and listening to reggae. The locals do not speak English and Keane's attempts at high school–level French make them laugh, but we get by. Queenie allows a group of children to bury her in the sand. When they've finished, she gets up and shakes sand everywhere, making them laugh and scream.

"This boat needs a name," I say when we're back aboard the Alberg that evening. "What about . . . *Braveheart*?"

Keane crinkles his nose. "As in William Wallace? 'They'll never take our freedom'? That's a bit . . . Scottish. Of course, it's your boat. Far be it from me to tell you what to do."

"Yeah, you've never done *that* before."

He laughs. "Whatever you choose will be perfect."

"As long as it's not *Braveheart?*"

"Exactly."

I shift, straddling his lap to face him, kissing his mouth as I telegraph the message with my hips that I want him. "Doesn't need to have a name right now."

"No." This time his laugh has a sexy, wicked edge and his lips are against my neck when he says, "No, it does not."

There are other boats in the harbor, but the boom tarp is low enough that we don't bother going down into the cabin. Keane rolls on a condom and I take off my bikini bottoms. No foreplay. No sweet words. Just need against need, fast, hard, and gasping. And when it's over, I press soft kisses all over his face and whisper with each one that I love him.

The difference between Keane and Ben, I am realizing, is Keane belongs to me in a way Ben never did. Ben loved me, but he always had an exit strategy. Keane is mine for as long as I want him. I can feel it in everything he says, everything he does.

tiny fissures (28)

Our time in Martinique feels endless as we spend days exploring every part of the island.

We pack the tent and drive up to Presqu'île Caravelle, a peninsula on the east side of the island with a wild coastline and an abundance of surfer beaches. We search for the dive shack where Keane met Felix and Agda, but find only the abandoned husk, reclaimed by nature, the rafters inhabited by swifts. We camp on the beach for the night and spend the next day learning—or relearning, in Keane's case—how to surf.

Another day we drive to Saint-Pierre, a town destroyed in 1902 by the eruption of Mount Pelée. A portion of the ruins remain, foundations of buildings dragged into the sea. Sainte-Pierre is a much smaller town now, having never fully recovered, many of the buildings boarded shut and a Catholic cathedral standing empty. I am reminded of Montserrat. Of how inconsequential my problems are in comparison. I'm a visitor who gets the best of paradise instead of the worst.

We are into our twelfth day on the island before we bring up the subject of leaving.

"Let's not," Keane says over breakfast in the cockpit. "We can squat in the dive shack. Fix it up. Raise some chickens and goats and grow our own vegetables."

I smear guava jelly on a slice of baguette. "Okay."

"You're an easier sell than I thought."

"I love Martinique," I say. "And not just because of the sex."

"No, but I'm always going to have the best memories of this island now."

Being with Keane is effortless. There's no guesswork involved with his moods, and I love how often his heart comes out of his mouth. I smile. Tell him to shut up, even though I love every word. He turns on the VHF and we listen to the weather forecast on a station broadcasting from St. Lucia.

"Our window is now," he says. "Otherwise, we'll get the front and have stay two or three more days."

"I want to stay anchored here in this harbor forever."

"What about Trinidad?"

At some point, Trinidad fell so far off my radar that I almost forgot about it. Following Ben's course doesn't matter so much anymore, but I need to see this trip through to the end. I need the closure. The only way to free ourselves from the tractor beam of this island is to go. I sigh. "Let's leave in the morning."

We take a long afternoon nap in the hammock. We buy a

fat lobster for dinner from one of the local fishermen, and after the dishes are washed, I play with Queenie on deck while Keane checks his email.

"Anna." There's gravity in his voice, but light in his eyes when he looks at me. "I've been offered a spot aboard a sixty-five-footer during Barbados Sailing Week with an eye toward becoming permanent crew."

The corners of his mouth twitch, wanting to smile, and as Queenie drops the ball into my lap, I consider how to respond in a way that won't reveal the tiny fissures in my heart. Keane and I have talked so much about doing something new, something together, but this is his dream. He's trying not to let it show, but he wants it. "That's excellent."

"And yet I'm not really getting a happy vibe."

"I am happy." Except there's a catch in my chest at the thought of him leaving. "This might be the break you've been waiting for."

He nods. "The owner wants me to join them for the round-the-buoys portion of the regatta, then do the Barbados to Antigua distance race."

His excitement is too big to be contained, and his smile makes me wonder if this is the last smile his other girlfriends saw before the wind gods carried him away. I blink, trying to hold back tears. I feel foolish for thinking he belonged to me.

His smile falters. "You're crying."

"Yes, because I'm selfish." I scrub my eyes with the heels of my hands. "I let myself believe we were going to build something together. I hoped that maybe I was enough to make you want to stay."

"You are, but—"

"The worst part is that you don't have to explain. I understand."

"Come with me," he says. "We'll sail to Barbados together and you can explore the island while I'm racing."

"What happens when you leave for Antigua? Or when the owner wants you to stay on for Key West or Tasmania or Dubai? Barbados was not part of Ben's plan, and it's certainly not part of mine."

"This doesn't have to be the end, Anna," Keane says. "I'll come back."

"When?"

"I . . . I don't know."

"I can't be your contingency plan," I say. "I have a victory lap to do on a beach in Trinidad, and even though I love you more than I could have ever imagined, I can do this without you."

"So, what are you saying?"

"That we both have somewhere we need to go. If we're meant to be together . . . we'll find our way back."

When he kisses me, I sink into it because kissing him has become as natural as breathing. When he is inside me, my body begs him to stay when my words don't. Later, when he is asleep, and I am on deck alone in the dark—his scent lingering on my skin and the echo of his fingers in my hair—I cry myself to sleep.

* * *

We're pretending that everything is okay as we walk the length of the town jetty to the open doors of Saint-Henri for Sunday Mass. I tell Keane I want him to be happy. That I don't want him to live with regret. That we'll never be more than a phone call or email away. But the lie in the middle is that I want him to change his mind. I kneel in the pew beside him, listening to him recite the prayers he knows by heart, and I pray for a miracle.

Again and again I stop myself from asking him to stay. It would be selfish. He is selfish. I am selfish. To the point where we cancel each other out, and we're just humans, bumping along the dark walls of our lives, feeling for the switch that will give us light. Hoping we don't fuck everything up.

When it's time for Keane to go, he takes the rental car. He kisses me a million times on the jetty. Until he has no more wiggle room to get to the airport on time.

"I love you, Anna." He kisses my forehead and it's almost my undoing. "I hope you know that."

"I do. I love you too."

I don't watch him drive away. I walk down the jetty and motor out to the Alberg without looking back. In some ways, I am back where I started—alone and miserable—but I am also changed. Stronger. Unafraid. Maybe Keane and I will be together someday, but I won't lose the ability to function at the loss of him. And if that's the legacy of our relationship, that is enough.

pirate queens (29)

I come out on deck the next morning to new neighbors—a large catamaran and a fifty-foot charter sailboat—and settle into the hammock with guava toast and my laptop. Among my emails is a note from my mother, complaining that Rachel and her brand-new boyfriend have already started talking about living together.

It's too soon, Mom writes, *but Rachel has never been very smart about men.*

I laugh. Maybe none of us are very smart about men. Except that's not true. Our timing may not have been perfect, but Keane was not the wrong man.

My mother doesn't need another thing to worry about, so I don't tell her I'm sailing alone again. Instead I fill my reply with Martinique, describing the slave memorial and the Mount Pelée eruption, the surfing and the camping. I take a picture of myself with Queenie, with Les Anses d'Arlet as our backdrop, letting her see that I am fine.

So she won't feel sorry for me, I withhold the truth from

Carla, offering the vague explanation that Keane had a job offer. I tell her I'm leaving Martinique soon, and that I should reach Trinidad in about a week. The finish line is so close. I have traveled more than 1,300 miles.

Queenie and I set sail at dusk. The breeze is stiff and the distance to St. Vincent longer than the crossing from Miami to Bimini—but I'm more confident than I was then, and my autopilot will give me some relief.

It's a little boring without Keane. I listen to music, finish the book I've been reading through the whole chain of islands, and put out a fishing line, but I don't catch a thing. While Queenie crunches her way through a bowl of kibble, I make myself a sandwich. I'm taking my first bite when I hear a rustling sound and look up to find the mainsail slumped on deck, blocking the companionway.

"Oh shit."

I scramble up the steps and push past the fallen sail. The boat is still moving, but at a slower speed with only the one sail. Nothing else is broken—just the halyard that holds up the main—but I can't climb the mast alone to fix it. And even if I could, I don't know how.

"What the hell am I going to do?" I ask Queenie. She tilts her head, unhelpful.

Keane would have a solution and I consider texting him, but I have no cell signal and I need to figure this out on my own. I need a makeshift halyard.

"Halyard. Halyard." I repeat the word over and over, as if saying it will manifest the answer. And it does. Because clipped to the lifeline is the spinnaker halyard.

I disable the autopilot, head the boat into the wind, and fasten the halyard to the top of the mainsail. The main doesn't go all the way up the mast, but it buys me enough sail area to get to St. Vincent.

St. Lucia slides past in the night and I sleep in twenty-minute increments, scanning the horizon for potential disasters before setting each alarm. Dawn bursts in pinks and yellows across the sky, and St. Vincent looms ahead of me. I am bone-tired and hungry, but happiness fizzes up inside me like a shaken soda bottle and I dance around the cockpit until Queenie barks. I pick her up and snuggle her.

"We did it," I tell her. "We are the pirate queens of the Caribbean."

Ben would be proud. Keane too. But most important, I am proud of myself.

* * *

The first St. Vincent boat boy, Norman, is lurking offshore in a little pink skiff as I lower the sail and motor toward Wallilabou Bay. He hails me on the radio, offering his assistance with mooring, and I radio back that I will take care of it myself. Undeterred, Norman runs up alongside the Alberg, insisting he can help.

"Throw me a line," he shouts. "I will take you to a mooring ball for just twenty EC."

"No, thank you." I try to keep my tone pleasant yet firm. Twenty Eastern Caribbean dollars is about $7.50. It's not an unreasonable amount, but I don't need help. Except Norman won't go away.

Another hail comes over the VHF, another boat boy, Justice, offering a guided tour of Wallilabou and the sites where some of the *Pirates of the Caribbean* movies were filmed. "After I help you moor, I can take you there."

"I am not interested, thank you," I respond, but he also comes out to meet me. They remind me of remora fish that swim with sharks, waiting for the flotsam that falls from the sharks' mouths, but I don't feel like the fearless predator in this scenario. Especially when Norman and Justice begin arguing with each other, their accents incomprehensibly thick and their boats drifting too close to mine.

A third skiff approaches, and a fourth, and they all clamor over one another to get my business, asking me to throw out a line, asking me to buy things, and peeking into my boat in a way that makes me incredibly uncomfortable. Norman grabs my lifeline, staking his claim over the others.

"Please take your hands off my boat." My voice gets lost amid their arguing. I reach into the cockpit locker and take out the flare gun. Load it. Climb up on the cabin top and scream, "I don't want a fucking mooring ball!"

The men go silent, their eyes round.

"I don't want a tour. I don't want a necklace." My voice is as big as I can make it, and I point the flare gun at the bilge of Norman's skiff. I would never fire it, but as long as he thinks I will, I have the upper hand. "I want you to take your hands off my boat and go away."

He pulls his arms up in a sign of surrender and makes an *I wasn't doing anything wrong* face at the others. These men are only trying to support themselves and their families, but their aggression is too much.

"All of you. Get the fuck away from me."

They mutter to one another as they leave. Look back over their shoulders as if they expect me to beg their return. Call me a crazy white bitch. My hands shake as I climb back down into the cockpit, turn the boat around, and motor away from Wallilabou Bay.

My eyelids are heavy with exhaustion—so tired, I could cry—but it's only four or five more hours to Bequia, the next island in the Grenadines chain. A hysterical laugh escapes me when I realize five more hours at sea no longer fazes me. I hug the coast of St. Vincent until I am calm enough to raise my jury-rigged sail and kill the engine.

* * *

The water in Admiralty Bay is so green and clear that I can see my anchor buried in the sand at the bottom. I dive in from the stern rail and Queenie splashes down beside me, dog-paddling in circles around me as I float on my back under the sun. My belly is filled with pancakes, and in the cool water, St. Vincent washes off me like sweat. We take a long nap in the hammock, go ashore to check in at customs, and stroll the Belmont Walkway, a narrow strip of pavement that runs along the seawall. We eat lionfish pizza at a little blue hut. And stop at Daffodil Marine Services to drop off my dirty laundry and hire someone to fix my halyard. Daffodil—a self-made businesswoman who raised her boat boy game to a marine service empire—guarantees both will be done by tomorrow morning.

Back on the boat, I doodle a sketch of me and my dog as pirate queens—Queenie with an eye patch, and me with crossed cutlasses behind my head—and write *State of Grace O'Malley* beneath. Long stretches of time pass without me saying a word. I sit with myself and am satisfied in my soul. Even missing Keane doesn't change that.

The harbor is lively with yachts, fishermen, and ferries from other islands, and a white woman from the nearest sailboat calls across the distance. She introduces herself as Joyce Fields from Port Huron, Michigan, and after I call my name back, she invites me to come have a drink. I put Queenie in the dinghy, and barely a minute later a glass of rum punch is pushed into my hand.

"Come, sit." Joyce is an apple-shaped woman wearing a strapless bathing suit that seems perpetually on the verge of falling down. Her tan is leather dark, and I wonder if my skin looks the same as hers. I don't know if it's because of the rum, the island, or a combination, but she is shiny-happy. "Where are you from, Anna?"

It's a simple question, but my home is right here, right now. "Florida, I guess."

She laughs. "You guess?"

"I'm kind of a nomad at the moment, but I started this trip in Fort Lauderdale."

"Goodness, you're so young." Joyce sounds like a concerned mom and it's very touching. "Did you come all this way by yourself?"

"I've done some of it alone, but I had company for most of the trip."

"We came up from Grenada," she says. "We took a couple of years to sail through the Caribbean, but we like the Grenadines and Grenada the best, so we've been going back and forth between the two for the past six months. What about you?"

"South to Trinidad, but I may keep going. Not right away because I need to save up some money, but—" I take a sip of punch, surprised at myself. Sailing to the Panama Canal would be incredibly difficult by myself, and I don't know that I want to cross the entire Pacific Ocean, but nothing is off the table. "Yeah. I can go anywhere."

I eat dinner with Joyce and her husband, Mike, who dinghies out from shore with a bucket of lobsters. The orange-shelled monsters send a pang of longing for Keane through me. I snap a photo and text it to him: What the poor folks are eating right now. I miss your face and the rest of you too. The three of us compare notes about islands we have in common, and I laugh at myself as the crazy screaming white woman of Wallilabou Bay.

"It's hard to choose a favorite," Joyce says. "But I think mine is Mayreau, just down the chain from here. Gorgeous beach, fun bars, and the national park at Tobago Cays is spectacular. Turtles everywhere. You can even swim with them."

I'm glad I've had enough rum to disguise the flush in my cheeks when I tell her Martinique is my favorite. It's not completely a lie when I tell her it's because of the slave memorial and the beach at Les Anses d'Arlet.

Before I go, Joyce takes my picture for her sailing blog and suggests we have lunch tomorrow. A warm buzz sits in my head, in my body, as I motor Queenie ashore for a quick bit of doggie business. I fall asleep with the hatch open to let in the stars, and dream about sea turtles.

* * *

Alexander from Daffodil's place shows up at dawn, bearing a bag of clean laundry and a replacement shackle for my halyard. I'm still trying to fully awaken when he scrambles up the mast and pulls the errant halyard back down to the deck. Within minutes the new shackle is installed. Alexander takes away my trash. I listen to the weather to make sure I have a window.

Joyce comes out on deck wearing her droopy bathing suit and holding a huge travel mug of coffee as I'm pulling up the anchor.

"You're leaving?"

"I need to swim with those turtles."

Her laugh drifts over to me. "Have fun. Be safe."

"You too. And thank you for dinner."

Before I'm out of range of the island's cell service, I check my phone to see if Keane texted back while I was sleeping, but there are no new messages.

The mainsail at full capacity, the boat powers through the water. I sail past Canouan and into the passage above Mayreau. I consider sailing to Salt Whistle Bay to see why Joyce loves it, but I want to swim with the turtles more. The ocean winds strengthen, so I put a reef in the mainsail until I get into the lee of the Tobago Cays. I lower the sails early and motor carefully, watching for the navigational markers that guide me through the reefs. There are about a dozen boats of all sizes and power sources moored off the beach of a tiny uninhabited island, and

I'm tying the boat to a mooring ball when a park ranger comes to collect the fee.

When I slip into the clear, shallow water and see my first sea turtle—almost close enough to touch, hanging in the water like a bird mid-flight—everything I did to get here was worth the effort. The turtle stares at me, and swims away. Underwater, time loses meaning as I follow my new friend, watching it dip toward the bottom and swoop to the surface, poking its head out into the dry world. I swim until my limbs are noodles and my stomach is ready to be filled.

Queenie brings me the ball to throw while I drink soup and eat a sandwich on the foredeck. I secure her in the V-berth for the night and fall asleep in the hammock, stretched under stars flung across the sky like confetti.

In my dreams, I am back in Fort Lauderdale, in my old apartment, with Ben's face hovering over me, his hips moving slowly against mine. His hair is soft between my fingers and I can feel him inside me. I'm startled out of the dream by my own voice, a moan, and I lie with my heartbeat racing. My body pulsing from a sleep orgasm. Tears of disappointment and guilt, happiness and confusion, fill my eyes. Especially when I realize that the way his body moved against mine was not Ben at all. It was Keane.

I give up trying to sleep when the first light appears on the horizon. It isn't bright enough to even call it sunrise when I raise the anchor and head south. I stop briefly at Union Island to clear out of the Grenadines and take Queenie for a walk. While she snuffles in a scrubby palm, looking for lizards, I text Keane: I hate that every part of me misses every part of you. As soon as I hit send, I regret it. Texting him isn't helping me move forward.

An hour later I am back under sail, aiming for Grenada, the last stop before Trinidad.

Dolphins accompany me for the first couple of hours, and with the autopilot engaged, I stand on the foredeck and watch them race the boat. These are common dolphins—a species I've never seen before—darker gray on their backs than the bottlenose variety, with light-colored sides. When they've had their fun, they disappear, and I'm left to fill the hours myself. I think a lot about my dream and second-guess whether I put Ben away too soon, fell too fast for Keane.

In Victorian times, rules of society dictated that widows wear black for a year and a day, then transition to half mourning, when they were allowed to lighten up their colors. Even if the widows' actual feelings were muddled, the rules were pretty clear. But my year and a day is coming up fast and I don't know what I'm supposed to do, let alone how I'm supposed to feel. There's no wrong way to grieve, but I've taken a step backward. I'm angry that Keane left, and angry Ben came back.

I put on dance music and push them both away. Sing at the top of my lungs. Pause to marvel that five miles away an active underwater volcano called Kick 'em Jenny is building an island. Thousands of years from now, a different woman might sail past alone; another people might settle there and make it a home. And, once more, Mother Nature puts my small life into perspective.

Sunset is imminent when I roll up the jib and lower the main to motor into the shelter harbor of Hog Island. Grenada resembles the other islands—green hills and golden beaches—and I'm nearing the mouth of the harbor when the engine alarm shrills. Queenie begins to howl, and I don't know what to do except turn off the motor. Down in the cabin, I pull up the companionway stairs and open the engine box. Heat blasts out at me, smelling like burnt paint. There's no fire, no smoke, but the engine definitely overheated.

"Shit."

This problem is more difficult than the halyard. I'm not capable of sailing into a harbor filled with boats, coming to a stop, and anchoring without a motor. And, unlike St. Vincent, where I'd have my pick of boat boys, there are none in Grenada. I consider calling for help on the radio, but pride pulls me back. Not knowing what has gone wrong on my own boat is embarrassing. On top of everything, it's starting to get dark.

"If I could take the dinghy ashore—oh my God! I know what to do! I know what to do!"

I fling open one of the cockpit lockers and grab a rope. Run up to the foredeck and tie the line to one of the cleats. Keeping hold of the line, I lower myself into the dinghy . . . and tow my boat into the harbor.

stranded in paradise (30)

I spend most of the next morning on the internet, troubleshooting what's wrong with the engine. I'm not sure I can afford a professional mechanic. I can only hope the fix is easy enough to do myself. Or maybe I can ask someone from a neighboring sailboat to help me. All signs point to the water pump bearing having seized up, so I take a local bus—a large van with about fifteen people squished inside—to the nearest marine repair shop in search of a new pump.

"We're waiting on a delivery boat from Trinidad," the mechanic tells me. "It'll be here Tuesday or Wednesday."

"Would anyone else have it, you think?"

He shrugs. "I can call around, but it's pretty unlikely."

"How much?"

"About three hundred US," he says. "Plus labor if you want us to install it for you. That will run about four hundred and fifty dollars with the service call."

I think back to Provo, when Keane and I decided not to spend extra money waiting for a weather window. Hindsight and a dislocated shoulder made it a bad call at the time, but now I have money for a water pump.

"Let me know when you get the part," I say. "I'll decide on the labor later."

Since there's nothing I can do until the water pump arrives, I decide to enjoy Grenada. I stop at the IGA in Grand Anse to restock the galley, then play with Queenie on deck while I cook up a pot of chicken, rice, and beans. Later, when music drifts across the water from the bar on Hog Island and a lively conversation from a nearby boat make the night too loud for sleeping, I swing in the hammock with Queenie.

`Your tool bag misses you too,` I text Keane.

I do it without thinking, and he doesn't answer, just like he hasn't answered my other texts. Maybe in the middle of the ocean my words get lost in space. Maybe a bag of tools is a small price to pay for Keane's escape. Doubt has a way of creeping into the smallest places and putting down roots, even though I don't believe Keane would ever leave that way. Even so, I need to stop doing this. I need to let go.

I email my mom and Carla to let them know I've reached Grenada. Celebrate crossing the 1,600-mile mark. Share my victories over the broken halyard and the failed engine. Attach the picture Joyce took of me in Bequia. I haven't devoted many words to describing the places I've been and the people I've met, but I'm saving them all for one big story.

Carla emails back almost immediately.

A—You look so different. And not just because you're
smiling. You look like the Anna I remember. I miss
you, but I love seeing how far you've come, both
geographically and emotionally. At the bar, we've been
keeping your progress on a map, but I know we've
missed some places in between. I can't wait to hear all
the details, especially the ones about Keane Sullivan,
because I've missed some details of that story too. Sail
safe. xoxo—C

Saturday, I take a bus to the market in St. George's, where I
wander a street lined with tent-covered stalls, heaping with vegetables and fruits, spices and souvenirs. I buy some fruits I've
never seen before—soursops, mangosteens, and sugar apples—
while vendors call out offers for T-shirts, tote bags, bottles of
hot sauce, and spice necklaces. Chicken-scented smoke swirls
around me as I drink the water from a coconut with a straw and
buy small sacks of spices for my mom—whole nutmegs, star
anise, cinnamon sticks, and tiny black seeds called nigella. I find
a blue batik sundress and a little steel pan drum for Maisie. And
I let myself be talked into buying three spice necklaces—strung
with red mace, cinnamon, ginger, clove, nutmeg, and turmeric—
for ten EC by a lady whose brown arms are draped with them.

"You hang it in the kitchen or the bathroom," she says. "It
lasts for three years and every six months or so, soak it in water
to freshen up the scent."

My last stop is at a meat vendor, where I buy some oxtail seg-
ments that I later cook with rice and beans and steamed cabbage.
After dinner I try one of the sugar apples, separating the knobby

skin into pieces. The white flesh is soft and sweet like custard, and each piece contains a seed. It's a lot of work for such a little fruit, but it's worth it. I wrap some of the seeds in a damp paper towel and stash them in a plastic baggie. Maybe I'll gather some dirt and start growing my own tree.

On Sunday afternoon a group of cruisers from all over the world load coolers of beer into their dinghies and raft them together off the beach in front of Roger's Barefoot Beach Bar, where a reggae band plays. I'm watching from the cockpit when a grandmotherly-looking white lady wearing a wide straw hat, corks dangling from the brim, motors past and shouts, "Come to the dinghy concert!"

I grab Queenie, a couple of bottles of Carib, and a bag of plantain chips, and join the party. I lash my dinghy to one belonging to a bald white guy in his late thirties. His dog, a shaggy reddish-black mutt, scrambles over the boats to meet Queenie before I've finished tying the knot.

"Sorry about that," he says. "Gus is a friendly guy."

"No problem. Queenie's glad for the company."

"I'm Dave." He reaches across to shake my hand.

"Anna."

"Where you from?"

"Technically Florida," I say. "But I belong to that boat there."

He laughs. "I like how you put it that way. So true. And get this . . . I belong to that boat over there."

I follow the line of his finger to a smaller, battle-scarred version of my boat with the name *Four Gulls* painted on the transom.

"Yours is the only other Alberg I've seen since I left Florida."

Dave explains that he spends most of his year in the Caribbean but works as a bartender back home in Cleveland every summer to feed his sailing habit. I tell him I ran away from home, and he laughs. After the dinghy concert, we give each other Alberg tours.

"Damn," he says. "Yours is so much cleaner than mine."

"Maybe. But I bet yours runs."

"What's wrong?"

"Pretty sure it's the water pump," I say. "The marine supply says they should be back in stock Tuesday or Wednesday."

"There are worse fates than being stranded in paradise," he says. "If you need a hand installing it, I'd be happy to help."

Dave admires my pirate doodle and when he sees the Polaroid from the patchwork house, he asks if Keane is my old man. I pretend to shake and turn over a Magic 8-Ball. "Cannot predict now."

He laughs. "Long distance can be a killer."

We go from my boat to his, cutting a slalom course through the anchorage and doing doughnut circles in the empty spaces between boats. We're laughing like little kids when an old guy comes out of his cabin to yell at us.

Four Gulls is crammed with stuff—power tools, extra sails, clothes everywhere, a broken fan clipped to the handrail—like a storage closet exploded. I have no idea how Dave fits himself and a dog in such a crowded space.

"I'd blame it on a rogue wave," he says. "But yeah. It's kind of a mess."

Taped to his bulkhead is a picture of him with a pretty blonde.

"Long distance?" I ask.

"Yup." He lifts a fist to bump and I tap my knuckles against his. "She'll be down in a couple of weeks. I'm going to have to start cleaning soon."

"You should probably throw everything overboard and start fresh."

He laughs. "Or set fire to the whole boat and use the insurance money to buy a new one."

Dave breaks out some Bud Light he brought from Ohio. We drink and play dominoes until sunset. He delivers me to my boat as anchor lights are going on all over the harbor. "Just like curfew," he says. "Give me a holler when you get your water pump."

I consider texting Keane as I crawl into my bed, but there doesn't seem to be much point. Even if the fault lies with the satellites, I've stopped hoping for a reply.

Monday, Queenie and I take a minibus to Grand Etang National Park, where we go for a long hike in the rain forest. Tuesday, I jump off a ledge into the pool at the bottom of the Annandale waterfall. Wednesday, the service manager from the marine repair shop calls to let me know my pump has arrived.

* * *

Dave comes over the following morning and talks me through each step of removing the broken pump and installing the new one. It doesn't take long at all.

"I'm pretty sure I've assembled IKEA furniture more complicated than this," I say.

"Exactly," he says. "Which is why it's ridiculous to pay for labor."

He double-checks to make sure all the bolts are as tight as they should be and gives me a thumbs-up. "You done good, kid."

With the engine repaired, the boat is ready for Trinidad.

I spend the rest of the day preparing meals for the crossing, so I won't have to cook if the weather gets rough. I clean the

244

cabin. Stow my gear. Rig up a makeshift kennel for Queenie in case she needs to be confined at sea. Dave comes by at dinnertime and takes me to his boat for a farewell burger. He grills them rare and dripping with cheese.

"Oh my God." I talk with my mouth full. "I can't remember the last time I had a cheeseburger."

"Right? I love seafood as much as the next guy," he says. "But I'll take an artery-clogging burger over fish any day of the week."

We tune into the weather report as we eat, and celebrate the prediction of calm seas with glasses of strong rum punch. Dave runs me back to my boat at dusk and gives me a farewell hug.

"We could exchange emails," he says. "But I don't really check my email that much."

"That's okay. I'm starting to understand that some people come into your life when you need them, and go when it's time," I say. "And, you know, if I ever have to replace the water pump again, I'll think of you."

He laughs and hugs me once more. "Have a safe trip."

I thank him. And it's time to go.

a million shimmering pieces (31)

Every so often the universe doles out rewards. Maybe for something as small as flossing every day or choosing paper over plastic. Or perhaps loving someone so much that it helps them stay alive a little while longer than they might have. For whatever reason the universe chose for me, I am rewarded with the most perfect night. A sky so clear that every star must surely be visible, and the moonlight is bright as it hits the water, shattering into a million shimmering pieces. It was daunting to cross the Gulf Stream two months ago, but tonight I'm not afraid of the sea. Not afraid of my future. Even if the wind kicks up and the waves build, I'm here for it.

The breeze remains constant and steady, and the night passes at the only pace it knows how. I use the autopilot to eat or go to the bathroom, but mostly I'm awake, one hand on the tiller. Somewhere between Friday and Saturday, I pass to the east of the oil rig platforms—two small bright cities in the middle of nowhere. The halfway mark. On the horizon, between the swells of waves, the lights of Trinidad begin to appear.

Traveling almost 1,700 miles might not have made an impact on mankind, but the crack in my own small world is patched. My happiness is too big to be contained. Queenie gives a contented sigh, her fuzzy chin resting on my thigh, and I'm suspended in a perfect state of grace.

Saturday arrives with golden light, rays of sun fanning out across the sky like a proclamation. The island looms bigger and greener the closer I get. Anticipation builds inside me. Trinidad is larger than most of the islands I've visited. It's more urban and developed, so I don't know what to expect here. About a mile offshore, I furl the sails, turn on the engine, and radio the coast guard on the VHF with my estimated time of arrival.

Venezuela and Trinidad reach toward each other with long, narrow arms of land, and the island-speckled strip of water separating them—the Boca del Dragón straits—is only about twelve miles wide. I motor between two small islands, Huevos and Monos, and into the harbor at Chaguaramas, a small industrial port on the northwestern end of Trinidad. Piers jut out into the harbor for oil tankers and dredges, and the marinas are forests of masts, filled with sailboats bearing flags from all over the world. The fishing fleet is clustered at the deepest part of the harbor, near dry-storage racks filled with powerboats. It's unlikely I'll hear back from Keane, but as I skirt the anchorage on my way to the customs dock, I text him anyway. Despite everything, he is the first person I want to tell.

I made it.

I spend a good portion of the afternoon cutting through the red tape of immigration, customs, and arranging a vet check for Queenie. The process is anticlimactic. I should be sipping champagne. Instead, once our papers are in order, I move the boat to a slip at a marina. I call my mom as I walk Queenie around the boatyard.

"I am so proud of you," she says, and I hear the smile in her voice. "Your identity was so wrapped up in Ben, I was afraid that this trip...Well, I thought you were going in the wrong direction."

"I probably was when I started, but not now."

"When are you coming home?"

"I'm not sure," I say. "I still have to decide what to do with the boat."

"You could sell it," Mom suggests. "Use the money to go to college or tide you over until you find a new job."

"Maybe," I say, but selling this boat is not even a consideration. It's my home. "Tell Rachel and Maisie hello and that I love them. Hopefully I'll see you soon."

I hang up and consider champagne or maybe having a fancy meal somewhere, but after twenty hours at sea, I'm tired. I lie down for a nap and don't wake up until the next day.

* * *

Sunday dawns with work to be done. Small things come first. I take a long, hot shower in an actual bathroom. I clean the boat. Do laundry. Stop at the grocery store, where I stock up on milk, eggs, cheese, and yogurt. I pick up an overdue bottle of champagne, a box of dog treats for Queenie, and a personal-size bag of M&M's—a luxury I haven't had since I left Florida—that I eat sitting in the grass of the boatyard while Queenie runs her legs to rubber. She flops down beside me, panting and dusty, and I tilt my face toward the sun. I wish Ben could see me. I wish Keane were here. But I'm starting to understand how sadness and happiness can live side by side within a heart. And how that heart can keep on beating.

While I sit, I watch a group of boatyard workers buying lunch from a bicycle vendor with *HOT DOUBLES* painted on the side of his cart. Curious, I brush the dirt from my hands and get in line, with no idea what I'm buying.

"Doubles is the national Trini food," one of the workers explains, spreading open his paper-wrapped lunch for me to see. "It's like a sandwich with two pieces of *bara*—that's the bread—and *channa* in the middle. Then you add sweet chutney or hot pepper or both."

I listen as the next guy orders a doubles with mango chutney, cucumber, and medium pepper. When it's my turn, I order the same and discover it's a bit like the West Indies version of a taco, but with fried bread that's filled with chickpeas. The mango is sweet, the cucumber cool, and even the small amount of hot pepper has more bite than I expected.

"Oh my God, that's so spicy!" My eyes water and my nose runs, making the locals laugh. I wash it down fast with a Red Solo soda.

"Maybe slight pepper next time," the first worker says.

"Definitely," I say. "Thanks for helping me order."

My lips burn and my hands smell like curry when I stop at the marine supply store in the harbor for the next thing on my list. The bigger thing. I buy a can of gold leaf paint and a small brush. Back on the boat, I spend some time on the internet, finding the right font.

I know so much more about my boat now.

Including the name.

With a damp towel draped over my head to keep the Caribbean sun from scorching the back of my neck, I balance in the dinghy, roughing out the letters—first with pencil, then painting them in. It takes a long time and my fingers start to cramp, but when I'm finished, the transom shines.

I change into a dress and wear the rough diamonds from Keane and stand on the dock beside the boat for my own private christening ceremony. Queenie sits at my feet, looking properly solemn, which makes me laugh as I pop the cork on the champagne bottle. I don't know how to christen a boat, so I simply ask the wind gods to bless everyone who ever sailed aboard this boat, including Ben. Especially Ben.

"And let any name this boat has ever had be stricken from your books and the new name hold favor in your hearts." I whisper the boat's name and pour a bit of champagne on the bow. "May this boat bring fair winds and good fortune to all who sail it."

I'm feeling pretty high, my insides bubbly with champagne, when I call Barbara Braithwaite. But before I can say a word, she cuts through the silence.

"The last time we spoke I was offended by what you said, the insinuation that I didn't respect Ben's choices," she says. "But . . . you were right. Charles and I wanted what we thought was best for him, never stopping to consider that he might want something else."

"I'm sorry I yelled at you."

"Maybe I deserved it."

"Maybe."

"Ben was my only child, my heart, and I—Well, when he died, I wanted to gather up all of his things and hold them close," she says. "When the lawyer told us about the boat—"

"You still can't have it," I say, this time more gently.

She laughs a little through her nose. "We're no longer contesting Ben's will. The boat is yours, along with some of the things in storage that I know he'd want you to have." Her voice breaks. "You made him happy for as long as he was able to be, and for that . . . well, I can't hate you. And believe me, I tried. Thank you."

"Thank you for sharing him with me, even when you didn't want to."

"Goodbye, Anna. Be well."

She hangs up, and one more door closes. I don't think I'll ever seen Ben's parents again, and I have no interest in visiting his box in the ground when he will always have a place in my heart.

My buzz has worn off when I get into the dinghy and follow the contours of the coastline to a secluded beach in Scotland Bay—the one where Ben and I were going to get married. Queenie leaps onto the beach and I drag the boat above the tide line to keep it from drifting away.

The sand is soft beneath my feet and I carry the box filled with photos from Ben's old Polaroid, the dried hibiscus flower from our first date, the handful of dirty-sexy love letters, and the suicide note.

I dig a pit in the sand with my bare hands and place everything inside, along with Ben's chart book. I'll have to buy a new one, but I have my own route now.

I strike a match.

Polaroids make little popping sounds when they burn. Tiny fireworks to mourn what might have been. Tiny fireworks to celebrate the life of someone I once loved. Someone I will always love.

I sit beside the fire—at the intersection of who I was and who I am—until the past is ash.

I bury the remains.

As I push the dinghy back into the water, my phone pings wildly in my pocket. I pause, worst-case scenarios running through my head. Mom had a medical emergency. Rachel was in a car accident. Something happened to Maisie.

Instead the screen is filled with a series of text messages.

```
I want you.
I need you.
I miss you.
I love you.
I am coming home.
```

state of grace (32)

I emerge from the cockpit the next morning, a little hungover and squinting into the sunshine, to find Keane Sullivan standing on the dock beside the transom of the boat. He looks at me with tired eyes and a face that's a mess of stubble, but trying to keep from smiling at him is like pushing against a wave. When our smiles meet, my heart does a joyful dance behind my ribs and oh Jesus, do I love this man.

"*State of Grace.*" He glances at the words painted on the back of the boat. "It's a beautiful and fitting name for your boat."

"Our boat," I say as he steps aboard and scoops up Queenie, whose entire body wriggles with happiness. I know exactly how she feels. She licks his chin and jumps out of his arms. "Shouldn't you be on your way to Antigua?"

"I should, but after the last race, I booked a flight."

"How was the regatta?"

"It was everything I'd hoped." He exhales. "It was great, Anna.

I was at the top of my game. Like the accident never happened. But . . . it wasn't enough. I mean, if you're not there at the finish, what's the fucking point?"

I close the space between us and kiss him hard. Before I can pull back, his fingers are on my face and in my hair, his mouth seeking forgiveness and mine granting it. He whispers he loves me, I whisper it back, and we kiss until we are breathless. Smiling. Our foreheads touching.

"Now what?" I ask.

"Well, I spoke to my friend in Florida about getting my US citizenship, and he offered me a position teaching sailing to people with disabilities," Keane says. "And Jackson Kemp has offered seed money for when we're ready to start our nonprofit."

"Really?"

"Something to do with being called an arse in Saint Barths."

I laugh. "I had no idea fundraising would be so easy."

"But for right now, Anna," he continues, "all I want is to stop chasing after things for a bit, and sail. I don't care where, only that I am with you."

"I love the sound of that." I step through the companionway and climb down into the cabin. Keane follows. "So, you should know that, while you were gone, I learned a few things."

I reach for his T-shirt, pulling it up and over his head. He shivers as my fingers skim his sides. "First, swimming with sea turtles is one of the best things in life. Ever."

He works open the buttons on my shirt and kisses my collarbone. "Turtles. Okay."

"Second"—I let my shorts drop to the floor as he watches—"replacing a water pump is easier than it seems."

"I'm going to save my follow-up questions about that for later," he says, hooking his fingers into the waistband of my bikini bottoms.

"And third, I can live without you."

"I, um—" His hands fall away, and he runs his fingers through his hair, eyebrows pulling together in confusion. "I don't know what to say to that."

"You don't have to say anything. Because fourth, I don't ever want to do it again," I say, reaching for the top button on his jeans. "So, the next time you leave me, Keane Sullivan, you'd better have a round-trip ticket in your hand."

Days later, we motor out of Chaguaramas and head north, the entire Caribbean archipelago ahead of us. I raise the mainsail while Keane consults our new chart book. "Where would you like to go?"

There are islands we missed on the way down—Mayreau, Saba, Nevis, Tortola—that I would like to visit, or we could return to the places we love. We could do both. We have no timeline. No schedule.

I step down into the cockpit and sit beside him on the bench. Queenie creeps onto my lap. The destination really doesn't matter. "You choose."

Keane considers, and flashes me a grin so roguish that I wonder what devil's bargain I've just made.

"Tell me, Anna," he says, slipping on his sunglasses and adjusting our course. "How do you feel about sailing to Ireland?"

ACKNOWLEDGMENTS

Advice givers always tell you to write the book you want to read. For me, this is it. I started working on it about eight years ago, so there are a lot of people to thank along the way.

The last person I usually mention is my husband, but Phil's sailing knowledge is reflected on every page, so this time he needs to be first. Thank you for answering my endless questions and not cringing too much when the characters made bad choices. I'm sorry I cut your cameo role, but you'll always be my star.

I am so thankful to have Kate Testerman as my agent. Her faith in this story never wavered. More than once she picked me up, dusted me off, and then went on to find the very best editor.

And having Vicki Lame as my editor feels like winning the lottery. I knew Anna and Keane would be safe in her hands—and they were. It's been an incredible experience, Vicki, thank you.

In fact, everyone at St. Martin's Griffin has been so excellent, especially Jennie Conway, Kaitlin Severini, Chrisinda Lynch,

Cathy Turiano, Marissa Sangiacomo, Naureen Nashid, Meghan Harrington, Marta Fleming, Kerry Nordling, and the creative services team. Thank you all for your dedication in bringing this book into the world.

Adam Finnieston and Elizabeth Pla of Prosthetic Orthotic Designs, Inc., answered all my questions about prosthetics and their care. Any inaccuracies are solely mine.

I don't know where I'd be without my critique partners, Su-zanne Young and Cristin Bishara. They're like opposite sides of a coin; Suzanne is my biggest cheerleader, while I can always count on Cristin to say, "Yeah, but, what if . . ." And I'm so fortunate to have both.

I'm also lucky to have a bunch of talented writer friends whose opinions have been invaluable, including Kirsty Eagar, Annie Gaughen, Kelly Jensen, Miranda Kenneally, Elisa Ludwig, Amanda Morgan, Wendy Mills, and Veronica Rossi. Thank you all, not only for sharing your time but also for your friendship.

It's not an exaggeration to say I had a *ton* of beta readers over the past six years: Carla Black (yes, she's named for you), Taylor Cote, Christina Franke, Anna Hutchinson, Cee Jay Maxwell, Sarah Moon, Pam O'Neal, Marissa Davis-Orban, Ginger Phillips, Stephanie Pierce, Grace Radford, Jessica Sheehan, Andrea Soule, and Gail Yates (you have dibs). If there is anyone I missed, please know it was not intentional. Thank you all.

Talking to Dave Welch about his Alberg 30, *Four Gulls,* was supposed to be for research purposes only. His enthusiasm was so contagious we bought one of our own. Thanks, Dave.

Terry Igo answered a bunch of questions about wills, estates, and trust funds. Even though most of it didn't end up on the page, he went the extra mile and I appreciate it.

It would be impossible to name all the wonderful people we've met in the islands who contributed to this story in large and small ways, but love and special thanks to Shelley and Phillip at Little Cocoa in Grenada; Njomo in Salt Whistle Bay, Mayreau; and Andréa and Lovan in Les Anses d'Arlet, Martinique.

Finally, thank you to Caroline, Scott, Mom, and Jack for listening (or at least pretending to listen) when I ramble on about imaginary people. You're the best and I love you all.